A WILLIE BLACK MYSTERY

GRACE

OTHER NOVELS BY HOWARD OWEN

Littlejohn
Fat Lightning
Answers to Lucky
The Measured Man
Harry and Ruth
The Rail
Turn Signal
Rock of Ages
The Reckoning

WILLIE BLACK SERIES
Oregon Hill
The Philadelphia Quarry
Parker Field
The Bottom

A WILLIE BLACK MYSTERY

GRACE

HOWARD OWEN

THE PERMANENT PRESS
Sag Harbor, NY 11963

For information, address:
   The Permanent Press
   4170 Noyac Road
   Sag Harbor, NY 11963
   www.thepermanentpress.com

Library of Congress Cataloging-in-Publication Data

   Owen, Howard, author.
     Grace : a Willie Black mystery / Howard Owen.
     Sag Harbor, NY : Permanent Press, [2016]
     Series: Willie Black mystery
     ISBN 978-1-57962-434-7
        1. Missing children—Investigation—Fiction. 2. African
   American boys—Fiction. 3. Mystery fiction.

PS3565.W552 G73 2016
813'.54—dc23   2016022816

Printed in the United States of America

To Karen, as always

CHAPTER ONE

Friday, December 5

The security guard is drunk.

We don't let the police academy dropouts who protect us from our readers have actual firearms, but this one seems to have gone all BYOG on us. He's waving it around in the lobby, more or less daring Rita Dominick to fuck with him.

She's not backing down, for which, don't get me wrong, I respect her, but you've got to pick your spots. We're watching from the relative safety of the stairwell down the hall. The guard is weaving a little. Later the cops will find the empty pint of Ten High in his car.

"Maybe we ought to rush him," Mal Wheelwright says. Sally Velez, Handley Pace, and I turn and stare at Wheelie.

He shrugs.

"Just a thought."

Our publisher is maybe ten feet from the guard, seemingly intent on doing it the way she's seen it done in TV cop dramas.

"Come on," she says. "Give me the gun. You know you don't want to shoot me."

He damn well seems like he wants to shoot her. I remember the white college boy down in the Bottom, must have been two years ago about this time, who got accosted by two black kids still young enough to qualify for the juvenile court system but toting big-boy guns. The college guy was with two friends who had more sense than he did. When he stood his ground, holding nothing but his dick, and told them to go fuck themselves, the two boys allegedly just looked at each other like, "You want this one?" And then the smaller one, who turned out to be just shy of his twelfth birthday, blew a great big hole right through Mr. Go-Fuck-Yourself's nice leather jacket. Some people haven't been watching the cop dramas on TV, I want to tell Ms. Dominick. Some of them have been living their own dramas, and when in doubt, they just shoot your ass.

"I want some justice," he's already said three times. "They killed 'Tesian, and you all don't even care."

Outside, three police cars have rolled up, but nobody's in any great hurry to get in harm's way. The cops know a little more about self-preservation than Rita Dominick does. A crowd has gathered across the street.

We're all a little stunned. We figured that, the first time somebody came after one of us with a lethal weapon, they'd be gunning for the editorial department. I almost feel like pointing the security guard in the right direction.

We find out later that the guard, whose name is Belman Cole but who goes by Shorty, got our publisher's undivided attention by calling her in her top-floor office and telling her there was someone to see her downstairs. We came down because one of the secretaries, all of whom have now fled, called Wheelie after the guard pulled his piece. She told him there was a hostage crisis in the lobby. She said she thought Shorty had been drinking. Sally and I were in Wheelie's office, so we followed along. Handley Pace was coming back from a photo assignment when all hell broke loose, so he ran for the stairs to join our now-cowering party.

We wait in place, us by the stairwell, the cops outside the door now trying to get the guard to talk to them. Ms. Dominick finally seems aware of how close she is to being our second publisher in the last couple of years to meet Jesus early.

"What do you want?" our publisher asks again. I detect a hint of shakiness in her voice. She gets the same answer as she did before.

And then the penny drops. 'Tesian is Artesian. Got to be. Artesian Cole. The East End kid who's been missing.

I run back upstairs. Sarah Goodnight is looking out the window along with the rest of the newsroom. They've been told not to go near the lobby.

"The boy you're doing the story on," I say, out of breath from my little sprint. "I think we've got a relative of his downstairs."

She walks down with me and I fill her in. When we get to the first floor, she walks out before I can stop her.

"Sir?" she says to the guard, who turns toward her, still waving his big-ass gun. "You're here about Artesian?"

I dive and knock her to the ground. In the commotion, Rita Dominick finally does something smart and puts great distance between her and the guard just as the cops make their move. They wrestle the man to the ground. His gun, a .45, goes skittering across the marble floor, stopping beside the spot where I have Sarah pinned.

"Have you lost your fucking mind?" Sarah inquires as I roll off her.

I ask her the same question, then help her up and explain that I like her better without a big hole in the middle of her chest.

"Like being on the floor would have made it harder for him to shoot me?"

"Well," I explain, "that's how they do it on TV."

They have the guy handcuffed, so it seems like a good time to step up to the plate. They also find out that the gun is not loaded.

"Excuse me," I say as I try to get near him. One of Richmond's finest tells me to step back, but I get the guard's attention.

"You were asking about Artesian? Artesian Cole?"

The guy just glares at me. He's being hauled away when he starts talking.

"You all don't care nothin' about 'Tesian," the guard says. He's in tears. "He been missing a week, and you all ain't wrote diddly about him. I asked that reporter, the one that did the story on him being missing, and he hung up on me."

Yeah, that would be Baer. Mark Baer did the original story, six days ago, about the boy going missing. It was B1 for a day and then disappeared as the cops failed to make any headway in Artesian Cole's disappearance. Sarah has been assigned to do some kind of follow, but obviously nothing's been written yet, hence the little performance this afternoon.

Hell, it was the East End. Kids disappear on the poor side of town. Shit happens. Families there usually don't have the clout to get the publisher's attention. Sometimes, it takes a gun.

Baer is not famous for treating callers with respect. Trouble with that is, if you blow people off enough, one of them will get a lethal weapon and try to teach you some manners, which is what Shorty Cole, who turns out to be the missing boy's uncle, did today. And, as in this case, they hardly ever go after the right person. While many of us, in the last year, have fantasized about Rita Dominick's demise, it hardly seems fair that our new publisher almost earned a toe tag because of Mark Baer's dickishness.

Now that the newsroom people are free to come down, two dozen or so filter in to find out what they missed. It's three o'clock. This whole thing took maybe twenty minutes. Seemed a lot longer.

I'm surprised that the rest of the staff didn't come down. And then I realize that this is the staff, or the part of it that's still here on Friday afternoon. Maybe ten years ago we'd have put a reporter on the case of a missing ten-year-old black kid from Gilpin Court. Maybe.

Our publisher, looking like the events of the recent past have drained all the tanning-salon glow off her, walks up to me. She's standing beside me, looking off into the distance.

"That was pretty gutsy," she says, quiet enough that no one else hears her, "jumping in there to try to save Sarah."

She pauses.

"What I want to know is, were you just going to let him shoot me?"

I hesitate.

"Well, the gun wasn't loaded."

"Don't worry," she says. "I don't hold it against you. I hold a lot against you, but not that. One of these days, I'm going to get my ass killed by not knowing when to back down."

We've had our ups and down, Ms. Dominick and I. She would have fired me last year for disobedience if I hadn't pulled a trump card and maybe entertained our readers for a few days with my too-first-person account of the demise of a serial killer. She'd probably pop a bottle of champagne if she could get rid of me without hurting "the product," which is what she calls our once-proud newspaper. Put it this way: I haven't built up a lot of goodwill points with our publisher, but I do respect her for facing down a guy with a gun. She's got balls.

Sarah comes over, now that the drama has washed over her.

"Thank you. I'm an asshole," she says.

I tell her not to talk dirty.

"Maybe I can find a way to show my gratitude for your chivalrous gesture," she says, either a smile or a smirk trying to break through.

"I told you not to talk dirty."

I have time to run by Laurel Street before punching in for the fun and games that is night cops. This is my second tenure as our paper's after-dark police reporter. If you don't fuck up, you only have to do it once. I am fifty-four years old, which is middle-aged only if you are very optimistic, and this crap does get old sometimes, but my options are somewhat limited.

I find a place almost in front of my mother's modest abode on Laurel Street. Growing up in various places in Oregon Hill, sometimes I had a stepfather or some other form of surrogate "dad" for a while. Usually, though, I was luckier, and it was just me and Peggy.

At seventy-two, Peggy Black is living proof that marijuana won't necessarily kill you. She is trying to cut back now that my darling Andi is living with her, along with the newest member of the family, my grandson, the handsome and brilliant William Jefferson Black, now six months old. They named him partially after me, sort of. They didn't go for Willie Mays Black, which is a blessing. Jefferson is a family name. The Blandfords, of whom the baby's father, Thomas

Jefferson Blandford V, aka Quip, is a dues-paying member, go for family names, even if they do have to borrow them from famous Virginians.

And, of course, you have Awesome Dude, who came in out of the cold and never left. Since Peggy lost Les Hacker to a better world, it's been a comfort to her to have the addled, but well-meaning Dude around.

"I just heard about that crazy shit at the paper," Peggy says by way of greeting. I wonder what kind of vocabulary my grandson is going to have. "Why didn't you call us?"

I am pleased to smell only a hint of weed in the air.

Andi is getting ready for her latest job, tending bar at one of the places that are springing up on a part of West Broad that was somewhat uninhabited in the near past. My daughter looks a little haggard, but no more so than any other single mother. Maybe less than most. Peggy and the Dude seem to be capable of caring for an infant, against all previous indications. I even come over once in a while (well, a lot) to help out.

I kiss Andi and ask her if she's getting her monthly checks from young Quip.

"Oh yeah. He's good at that. Him and his family would do a lot more, if I'd let them."

The Blandfords have been known to come by Peggy's on occasion. One explanation would be that they want to spend quality time with their grandchild, even if he doesn't share their last name. The reason I go with, though, is that they're angling for some way to get William into the bosom of the Blandford household and give him the West End upbringing one springing from their loins so richly deserves.

"They act like they smelled something bad when they come here," Peggy says.

Maybe, I suggest, it's the dope. Maybe that's a good reason to cut back a little, or a lot.

"It's got so bad I got to smoke in the backyard, like it was tobacco or something," she says, casting aspersions on one of my vices.

Everything returns to normal, or what passes for news-room normal on a Friday evening in the early twenty-first century. Most of the staff has left the building, having put in their thirty-seven and a half hours or maybe luxuriating at home on one of their unpaid "furlough" days.

No new bodies have surfaced in the city. I'm working on a story about the murder rate in Richmond in 2014, leaving room to update for those last-minute Christmas homicides. Sarah is working on that story about Artesian Cole, now that his family has our attention, getting whatever noninformation she can from the police. I give Peachy Love a call at home, hoping to get some inkling of what, if anything, the police know about the boy's disappearance.

"Yeah," she says, "I heard about all the to-do over there at the paper today. Made me sorry I opted for the quiet life of law enforcement."

Pechera Love used to be a reporter for us before she chose more dependable employment as a police flack.

She asks me when I'm going to come by and see her. I'm pretty sure she means "see" in the Biblical sense. I tell her I have to get permission from my lady friend.

"Well," Peachy says, "I don't want to mess up a good thing. It's nice that you're not afraid of commitment. Get right back on that horse."

Peachy is making a somewhat catty reference to my spotty—OK, piss-poor—record with matrimony. Hey, it takes two to make a divorce. I've just chosen poorly. Three times. I'm not sure that Cindy Peroni, a one-time loser herself, wants to take a chance on the fourth time being a charm. And I'm not sure I want to put her through the Willie Black experience. When people ask me, I just tell them we're going steady.

Peachy says she doesn't know anything else about the case.

"His mother said he was going to that tutoring program over on West Grace, CHOG or whatever."

Children of God. We already knew that. Sam McNish has been running that program for years. He's one of Oregon Hill's shining stars. We do a story on him every once in a while, on how he's trying to save Richmond one kid at a time. He's eight years younger than I am, and I don't really know him, but I don't trust anybody who works that hard at doing good. Call me a cynical newspaper bastard (take a number), but I've seen too many angels fall from heaven.

"And that's it? Nobody else saw him?"

"Nobody that's talking to us."

I ask her how hard the cops have been trying.

I hear her sigh.

"You know how hard, Willie. About as hard as you all have been pursuing it at the paper. Maybe that mess today will put it on the front burner."

Between my African American father and Peachy's full-fledged membership in the minority world, we do know how it works. But it isn't just about color. We've been known to discriminate against poor people of all creeds and colors.

"Well," I say, "call me if you know something. And I will get by sometime, I swear."

"Right," Peachy says. "Soon as you get that permission slip."

NOT MORE than an hour later, Peachy calls, interrupting my online solitaire.

"They found him."

"Him or his body?"

"His body."

Little Artesian Cole's corpse bobbed to the surface in the lake over at Bryan Park, over by where they play Frisbee golf, the only sport I know that makes golf seem sensible by comparison. Apparently the body had been put in a sack, weighted down with bricks, but somehow it had worked loose.

Sarah and I go hauling ass over there. At the scene, I spot Gillespie, one of the few cops who will speak to me. The fat bastard tells me, loud enough for his compatriots to hear, that it's a crime scene and I need to step back.

When we're away from the swarm of law enforcement folks who have descended on the lake, he gives me a few crumbs, more or less out of the corner of his mouth. Larry Doby Jones, Richmond's police chief, and I are in at least an uneasy truce at present, but Gillespie knows you don't get points with the boss for cozying up to the man Jones has referred to in the presence of witnesses as "that big-nosed son of a newspaper bitch."

Artesian Cole was in the fifth grade. He was an honors student, which in some parts of our fair city does not qualify you for Mensa. But he was in McNish's after-school program, and his mother told the cops that they thought they could get him into some kind of gifted program, maybe even get him in Governor's School when he reached high-school age, which he never will.

As we already knew, he never showed up at home after leaving McNish's program on West Grace the day he disappeared.

Gillespie pulls me farther out of the light. He wants some information from me for a change.

"What do you know about that guy, McNish? He's from the Hill, too, right?"

"He's eight years younger than me. I never knew him, just heard about him after I went to work for the paper. The home folks think he walks on water."

I ask him why he wants to know.

Gillespie gets all evasive, the way he does when he actually knows something for a change.

"Nothin'," he says. "Just asking."

Bullshit, I'm thinking. But if Gillespie's heard something, Peachy Love will hear it soon, I'm sure. And then I'll hear it.

I walk over to where Sarah is standing. She looks a little shaky.

"Did you see him?" I asked her.

She nods.

Sarah subs on night cops often enough that she's been exposed to a few dead bodies. She's pretty blasé about stiffs these days. This one seems to have gotten to her a little, though.

"He was so small," she says. "He looked like he'd shrunk or something."

There was something else, she said.

"He was wrapped in a bedspread or something like that, but he looked like he was naked, underneath."

They're taking the body away by the time I go to take a look. I'm not supposed to, but sometimes it's better to ask forgiveness than seek permission. A quick peek before a young cop tells me to get the hell out shows me a shriveled little boy, all gray and ravaged by six days in the water. The dark stain all over the spread comes, I'm pretty sure, from bleeding out. There's no reason to look, but sometimes it's good to get a refresher in just how bad humans can be to each other.

"When it stops getting to you," I tell Sarah, "it's time to quit."

She nods and heads toward the chief, hoping for a statement.

The chief answers questions from the three TV reporters and Sarah.

"Are you treating it as a homicide?" one of the video hairpieces yells out.

The chief says they aren't treating it as anything yet. It is an ongoing investigation, which is L.D.'s answer to everything when he doesn't know anything else.

I don't believe the TV folks got here in time to get a look at the body.

I sidle up to the chief as he goes back to his car.

"That was blood all over that spread, wasn't it?" I ask him. "And he was naked underneath it."

He starts to give me some bullshit answer, then just nods his head.

"But you can't quote me on that."

I tell him that if he doesn't say anything, I can't quote him. I can just state the fact with no attribution.

"No what?"

"I won't quote you. I won't even say it was a police source."

"You got an answer for everything, don't you?"

I tell him that if I did, I wouldn't be working the damn night cops beat.

He actually laughs and tells me he better not see his goddamn name in our goddamn newspaper anywhere near a quote mark.

SARAH WRITES the story. And I've got one more homicide, I'm pretty sure, to add to our yearly list.

CHAPTER TWO

Saturday

It's beginning to look a lot like Christmas. The guy standing in the median at the first stoplight off the I-95 exit ramp is wearing a Santa Claus hat he must have found in somebody's trash bin. The cardboard sign he's holding reads "Will work for bear." I'm hoping he means beer.

I went back to the scene of our latest heinous crime this morning. There isn't much to see, just a crime tape still up, for some damn reason, around where they dragged the boy's body out. I thought it would be good to get a little background. Tug at the readers' hearts, or at least give them a chance to wonder out loud over breakfast what makes "those people" do things like that. It's always good to humanize the end-of-the-year murder recap. We don't have as many homicides as we did when crack was king, but we do well enough to keep the suburbanites from coming into town after dark. Even with our reduced carnage, I don't have enough time to focus on every drug-related dirt nap on my plate. This, though, was ridiculous enough to make me go the extra mile. Artesian

Cole was, by all accounts, a great kid, good student who did everything right. It kills me how much more likely it is that something like this will happen to a good black kid than a good white kid.

The morning was not without event. I was standing there, slightly hung over and sucking on a Camel, getting the death stare from some jerk jogging by, like I might give Bryan Park cancer, when I saw them walking more or less in my direction.

The large, well-structured black woman was being helped along by a man whom she towered over. If she stumbled, she would have crushed him to death.

They got maybe twenty feet away when I recognized the guy, so I knew who the woman must be.

"Shorty," I said, and he jumped a little. He let go of the woman, who I knew had to be his sister.

"You're that guy from the paper," she said.

I confirmed that and noted that I was surprised to see Shorty out walking around. I didn't want to say the wrong thing and hurt his feelings, in case the gun was loaded this time.

"Oh," he said, "it wasn't no thing. We made the bail. Don't guess I'll be working at the paper no more though."

I nodded, full of heartfelt sympathy. Holding the publisher hostage probably will necessitate a job search for Shorty Cole, assuming he doesn't become a guest of the state soon. I told him that I'd be glad to give him a reference.

"It just makes me so damn mad," he said. "Didn't seem like nothing was being done. So I decided to get their attention.

"Oh," he added, realizing he'd forgotten his manners, "this here is Laquinta."

I expressed my condolences.

"I just wanted to see where they found him," she said. "Who in the world would want to do that to 'Tesian? Oh my Lord, he was my pride and joy."

She moved toward the water, and I was afraid she was going to throw herself in. Neither Shorty nor I, nor both of us, could have lugged her out.

But she stopped at the edge and started crying. Her wailing was such that a flock of geese on the other side decided to crap elsewhere. Who could blame her?

A good man would have left them to their grief, but I'm a reporter.

When she regained a little of her composure, I asked her if she had any idea at all who would have wanted to hurt her son.

She shook her head.

"He went to that Grace of God place after school every day, and he had to either get a ride or catch the bus back home, but nobody had ever bothered him. And that Mr. McNish treated him just like he was his son."

"We got to go, Laquinta," Shorty told her. "We got to make the arrangements."

She didn't seem like she wanted to leave there, ever, just stay where her son's body was brought up. Next stop would be the undertaker's, and she would know, even more than she did already, that nothing was ever going to be the same.

I stop at the Good Luck "convenience" store just past the light to buy cigarettes and a lottery ticket from a guy apparently trying to learn English by watching ESPN. The cigarettes no doubt will give me a lot more comfort than the scratch-off. The other people in here buying tickets are the ones that make the better classes call the lottery a tax on the stupid. Really, though, if you're having to buy your beers one at a time in a paper sack, Power Ball is about the only 401(k) plan you've got.

I heard a guy one time, in the act of not minding his business, tell a bedraggled old coot who'd just bought twenty bucks worth of MegaMillions tickets that his odds of winning were like forty-five million to one.

The old guy squinted up at his self-appointed investment advisor and said, "Son, my whole life has been forty-five million to one. This has got as good a chance of coming in as anything else."

Then he suggested that the guy go fuck himself. We all applauded. I gave the old guy five bucks and told him to go for the gold.

WHAT I want to do now is talk to Sam McNish.

I go back to the Prestwould and my sixth-floor abode. I'm still renting from Kate, my third ex-wife. We get along fine, now that we don't have to lie to each other about where we were last night.

I'm a little out of place among the essence of the kind of old Richmond where someone might actually ask you, "Who are your people?" Somebody did that to me once, at a cocktail party. I told her she really didn't want to know. But I genuinely like my neighbors here, and they tolerate me well enough.

Abe Custalow, to whom I'm subletting the second bedroom, is taking the afternoon off from his job as the Prestwould's maintenance man and has his ample frame hunkered down watching a little college football. I have a rare and blessed Saturday off, the better to take the lovely Cindy Peroni to dinner tonight. The couple of hours I spent tramping around Bryan Park on a nonworking day are my early Christmas gift to the paper.

"So what's the latest with that boy?" Abe asks.

I tell him there's nothing much new.

"I see he was one of Sam McNish's kids."

"Yeah," I tell him, scooping up some avocado dip with a tortilla chip and almost not spilling any on the carpet. "Funny how a guy from the Hill became our very own Mother Teresa."

Custalow frowns.

"Yeah," I say. "You're right. I'm a cynical bastard. It's just that I never really bought into any of that Jesus stuff."

"I don't think Jesus had much to do with it. I think he just wanted to do good."

I call the Grace of God number, but no one answers. I don't leave a message. Maybe I can catch him tomorrow.

LIKE ANYONE from Oregon Hill, I've heard the Sam McNish story so many times I practically know all the words. What I didn't know already, Cindy filled me in on when we started dating, going steady, hooking up, whatever the hell you call it these days.

He was, by all accounts, a nerdy little kid, brought up like yours truly by a single mother. Like me, he was an only child. Supposedly, his mother was some kind of West End society girl who fell in love or lust with a Hill boy who took her home, gave her his somewhat dubious name, and then left her. For some reason, maybe because she wasn't welcome anymore among the "Who are your people?" crowd, she didn't go back to the land of boxwoods and trust-fund babies. Like Peggy, she staked her outsider's claim on the Hill. She stayed. She was, by all accounts, determined that her one and only was not going to be some kind of juvenile delinquent, the norm on Oregon Hill. Studying was not optional in the McNish household.

Little Sam skipped the third and sixth grades and graduated from John Marshall High School as valedictorian when he was barely sixteen. He got a full scholarship to Princeton, and most folks on the Hill probably figured he'd seen about the last he wanted to see of Richmond as he headed north on the Amtrak.

Like any smart, undersized kid where we grew up, he reportedly got picked on a lot, for a while. The story they like to tell is about how he got even with Brady Stoneburner and stopped being fucked with.

Brady was a year older than Sam and, by all accounts, about a foot taller by the time they were in junior high. Brady, no genius apparently, had kind of balanced things out by repeating a grade to make up for one of the ones Sam skipped. The upshot was that Brady, a year older, was in sixth grade when Sam was in eighth.

Maybe this gave Brady Stoneburner feelings of inadequacy. Whatever, he decided to take it out on Sam McNish. He reportedly would come up behind him and knock his books out of his hands, or give him a friendly slap upside the head, or maybe just taunt him a bit, hoping that the smaller boy would make his day and give Brady an excuse to beat the crap out of him. But Sam didn't do anything, just took it.

One day, though, he took control of the situation. The way they tell the story, Brady was at his locker, probably trying to remember the combination, when Sam came up behind him.

"Hey, Brady," he said, "I got something for you."

Stoneburner turned around and came face to face with a rather healthy snake. It wasn't poisonous, most agree, just a good-sized rat snake young Sam had managed to sneak into Binford. Unknown to most of his classmates, Sam McNish had become quite fond of reptiles and didn't seem at all scared of them.

The same could not be said for his nemesis. Stoneburner is alleged to have actually managed to climb his locker and was found by the assistant principal sitting atop it with his legs drawn up. He was crying.

Before the assistant principal got there, Sam calmly explained to Brady that if he wasn't shown a little more respect in the future, he couldn't be responsible for what might or might not pop out of Brady's locker the next time he opened it.

"In other words," he said, according to Cindy, "don't fuck with me."

No one had ever heard Sam McNish cuss before. It made almost as much of an impression as the snake did.

A couple of idle threats by Brady Stoneburner followed, until the day Sam put the cobra in his chair. It wasn't real, of course, just a doodad they were selling at the Virginia Museum to cash in on some kind of Egyptian exhibit there. It was spring-loaded so that any little movement would make the cobra's head pop up like a jack-in-the-box nightmare.

That morning in English class, Brady came in, still no doubt with some of his strut intact. When he got to his desk and jostled it a little as he threw his books down, the cobra popped up, and Brady Stoneburner wet his pants. The rest of the class knew the fake snake was there, and the merriment was reportedly widespread. Attached to the snake's head was a note that read: "I told you once."

It is said that Sam got a couple of days' suspension for bringing a real snake to school and no time at all for the artificial one. Cindy said she figured the teachers and principal were as tired of Brady Stoneburner as Sam McNish was.

Other aspiring bullies kind of gave Sam a wide berth after that, Cindy said. Still, he didn't have a lot of close friends. For one thing, he was two years younger than the rest of his classmates. He supposedly didn't have a date until his senior year. But, the Brady Stoneburner incidents notwithstanding, he was reportedly a kind, considerate boy. He made a point of befriending the most friendless, including a couple of kids who had just enough Down syndrome to stay in the mainstream rather than being relegated to the short bus. His second date, the story goes, was to the senior prom. He brought a black girl from Carver who was just behind him in the class rankings and would go to Duke on a full scholarship. The general consensus was that they both did it just to jerk a few chains. Being half African American myself, I respect what it took to do that in Oregon Hill in 1982. Custalow and I had our share of Brady Stoneburners. We didn't have Sam McNish's imagination, though. Mostly, we just beat the shit out of them.

"We all respected him and admired him," Cindy said. "But he wasn't, you know, close to anybody much."

With all this in his history, it was a surprise to many when he moved back to Richmond. The reason, too, was something of a jaw-dropper. He'd graduated with honors from Princeton and had been accepted to law school at Yale. Instead, he came back here to go to Union Presbyterian Seminary. With all that education and all those brains, he was going to be a preacher.

It was seen as kind of an insult to many who had cheered him from afar, holding him up to outsiders as proof that growing up on the Hill didn't necessarily consign you to a life of manual labor or incarceration.

"He coulda been a senator or something," I heard a guy say one time at the Chuckwagon over a beer or six.

"Well," somebody else said, "he's doing the Lord's work."

"Hell," the guy said, "anybody can do the damn Lord's work." And then he had to apologize to the Baptist preacher who was sitting two seats down enjoying a cold one.

At any rate, he returned, and he never left again. The way he chose to employ his energy and brain cells is nobody's business but his own. Not my cup of tea, but that's just me. I've never been much of a churchgoer. Peggy tried to make a Christian out of me, but it kind of kills your want-to for religion when your only parent pushes you out the door in your Sunday best with a joint in her hand.

"You need to know that shit," Peggy said. "It isn't right for little kids not to go to church. You don't want to go to hell, do you?"

But it was plain to me, by the time I had reached the so-called age of reason, that Peggy wasn't buying much of what the preacher was selling. She would point out the bad things that the deacons and elders were doing Monday through Saturday before putting on their "Jesus suits" on Sunday. Bottom line, I don't think either Peggy or I have ever really swallowed the fact that you can be Adolf Hitler, or even the owner of the Dallas Cowboys, and undo a whole life of evil with a simple "my bad" on your death bed. It's just too easy, and nothing in Peggy's life, or mine growing up, caused us to think that you could believe in "easy." Where we came from, about the only thing that really worked was "hard."

I do credit Sam McNish with choosing to deal with the day-to-day, earthly needs of people as opposed to the harps-and-wings versus hellfire-and-brimstone tack many of my least favorite evangelists employ. Working with kids whose lives make mine and Custalow's on the Hill seem like *Leave it to Beaver* is to be admired, whether it's done by the church or the Mafia.

I try Sam McNish's number one more time and get no answer.

Five minutes later, I get a call from L.D. Jones.

This is unusual, to say the least. Most times, my calls to our police chief go unreturned. He has not, in my memory, ever called me other than to chew me out for doing my job, which sometimes inevitably involves making our chief and his minions look less than capable.

"I need some information," he says, by way of greeting.

I tell him that's what he's supposed to give me, not the other way around.

"Cut the bullshit," L.D. replies. "Can you meet me somewhere in an hour or so?"

I am intrigued. We agree on the new Perly's. I figured I have plenty of time. Cindy isn't expecting me until six thirty at least.

It's a ten-minute walk down Grace Street. Virginia Commonwealth University is creeping eastward from the Prestwould, but this part of Grace is still a little on the sketchy side, even with the police station perched halfway there.

I haven't dined at Perly's lately. Since it reopened, they don't serve pork, which pretty much eliminates any kind of breakfast I might ever order. Still it's nice what they've done to the place. I hear you can make sausage out of beef too. God, Cindy tried to slip some past my tonsils the other morning that was made out of soy.

L.D. is coming out of 200 West Grace and walks with me the rest of the way. We talk about the weather and U.Va. basketball and my smoking until we get inside to a back booth. It takes awhile. The chief likes to speak to his peeps, many of whom seem to still be patrons of Perly's despite its pork-free reincarnation.

He's ordered late lunch and I've ordered a Miller before he cuts to the chase.

"What do you know about this guy McNish?" he asks. "I mean, he grew up on the Hill, right?"

I tell L.D. that I know a little about him, but that he's a good bit younger than me. I tell him that, as far as I know, he's on the side of the angels. I ask him why he wants to know.

He gets all official on me, starts the usual bullshit about ongoing investigations and such.

I stop him.

"L.D., it's just me. You know I'm not going to print anything you say if it's off the record. But you've gotta shed a little light here. I don't like being in the dark. Little help, L.D."

He sighs and tells me what a pain in the ass I am.

"OK," he says, lowering his voice a little even though the booth next to ours is empty and the noise level in the place makes me have to lean halfway across the table to hear him. "Off the record, and I do mean off the record. He might have been the last person to see that boy alive."

He is, of course, talking about Artesian Cole.

"You mean, other than the asshole who killed him."

He looks at me.

"I mean what I mean. Now, can you tell me something about Samuel Jackson McNish?"

I tell the chief that I didn't even know that was his full name. Then I give him as much background as I care to.

"And he's never done anything that might indicate that he might, uh . . ."

"Murder one of the kids he's trying to help? Yeah, right."

I might be sneering a little when I say it.

The chief comes about halfway across the table, the better to make his point.

"Let me tell you something. You don't know shit. You see some dead bodies out there at night once in a while, and you think you know evil. You don't. I have seen it all. Last

month, some crackhead mother on the South Side sold her
little girl. Yeah, that's right. Sold her. Nine fuckin' years old.
We're pretty sure that's what happened, because that's what the
mother of the year's aunt told us when we found the skank
dead in an old boarded-up house over in Dogtown. We still
haven't found the girl. We might never find her."

He's resting his elbows on the table. I don't bother to
mention the ketchup on his sleeve.

"That boy," he says, "it looks like he might have been
abused, before he was killed."

I ask him the question I already pretty much know the
answer to. When a body shows up dead and naked, you
assume certain things.

"Sexually?"

He stares at me and nods.

"So don't get all wiseass on me. I didn't have to go to college to be an expert on the human condition. And the human
condition is pretty damn sorry. I expect the worst until I'm
shown otherwise."

It's as long a speech as I've ever heard L.D. give. My old
basketball buddy and present antagonist is definitely all in on
this one.

I promise him that I will check around, not mentioning
that I am having dinner and maybe, if I'm lucky, breakfast
with one of Sam McNish's former classmates.

He nods and motions for the check. I don't resist. My tax
dollars at work.

"There must be something," I tell him. "There's something
you're not telling me. Take me to the mountaintop, L.D."

He hesitates before he speaks.

"Again," he says, "off the record. Double off the record."

Another pause.

"There was a teacher's aide or some such shit at that Children of God place. She saw something."

"Something."

"She said he gave the boy rides home sometimes."

That seems innocent enough, I offer.

"She saw him and the boy coming out of the bathroom together one time. She said the boy looked upset, and when she asked if he was OK, McNish said the boy was fine, like he didn't want to talk about it."

"That doesn't sound like much."

L.D. sighs.

"It's all we got."

CINDY WANTED to go to one of the new places that keep popping up around here. If all the gastronomic palaces are as great as our restaurant critic says they are, I asked her once, how come most of them are gone in three years and Joe's and the Robin Inn are still here.

Cindy noted that there's always a market for a place where nine bucks will get you enough spaghetti for lunch and dinner, but sometimes people want a little swish.

Not me. But here we are. There are a lot of things with arugula and beets and carrots in them, and lots of items I only assume are food, but not so much red meat. We're supposed to share. How, I ask Cindy as she tries to divide a chicken thigh, is this different from a buffet, except it costs more?

Cindy has a sense of humor, which is what saves me. She thinks it's funny when I ask the waiter if the kale is free-range. Some of my other love interests have not been so tolerant of my irrepressible wit.

She is looking extremely fine tonight. It's worth making her smile to see those dimples. Her dark hair frames her face perfectly. Her eyes, those mischievous bedroom eyes, make me wonder how her former husband could have been asshole enough to let her get away. Unlike me, she is in exceptional shape. I can't believe she's forty-eight years old. Looking in the mirror in the men's room, however, it is very easy for me to believe I'm fifty-four. Hell, I have the looks and stamina of a man of sixty. Maybe 2015 will be the year I run the Monument Avenue 10K. I mentioned that possibility to Cindy last week.

She snorted.

"You crack me up," she said. "Oh, wait. You're serious?"

I told her not really.

"You know," she said, "they won't let you smoke during the race."

Dinner goes well, with a minimum of sharing. A couple of obscenely expensive bourbons on the rocks and a bottle of a very passable Italian red help my digestion, although I'm afraid the bill is going to give me acid reflux.

We eventually get around to the subject of Sam McNish. I don't mention the fact that L.D. Jones has taken an unhealthy interest in her old classmate.

"That thing with the boy was so sad," she says. "I hope it won't keep other kids from coming to that program. I hear he's doing a lot of good."

"It's got to make people a little leery," I offer.

"Well," Cindy says, "there's kids out there who are behind before they come out of the womb. I think Sam's just trying to help them catch up."

I ask her if she ever sees him.

"Yeah," she says, "I have, although not lately. When my marriage went south, I volunteered over there for a while, until I started taking courses at VCU."

I haven't heard this before. I tell her that she continues to surprise me with all the nooks and crannies of her life.

"Oh," she says, as the dimples reappear, "I think you're pretty familiar with my nooks and crannies."

I call for the check. I mention that it seems like a good time to go home for the evening.

"You want to call it a night?" she asks me.

"No. I just want to go home for the evening. Yours, I hope. Unless you want dessert."

The dimples again.

"That's all right. We can have dessert at my place."

Cindy and I have had some ups and downs, the downs mostly my doing. But we've done the things couples do when the good outweighs the bad. We overlook each other's faults. She overlooks my drinking and smoking and flirting. I overlook the fact that she is so adorable she can't possibly put up with me for much longer.

CHAPTER THREE

Sunday

"Willie," Cindy says, punching me the way she does when she claims I'm snoring, "it's your phone."

I fish it out of my pants, which are lying balled up beside the bed.

"Sorry to, uh, wake you up," Custalow says, "but we had that breakfast thing. Want me to go on and you catch up later?"

I forgot that I had promised R.P. McGonnigal and Andy Peroni that Custalow and I would join them at the Bamboo for an Oregon Hill catch-up.

Cindy seems amused at my efforts to wake up and get dressed simultaneously.

"Your pants aren't zipped," she points out as I get ready to leave. I reach down to kiss her.

"I've got morning mouth," she says. She tries to turn away. I tell her that's because it's morning and kiss her anyhow.

"So you're meeting Andy for brunch?"

"We prefer to call it breakfast."

"Well," she says, dimples at full mast, "don't tell him what a slut his sister is."

"My lips are sealed."

"Maybe they should be, until you brush your teeth."

THE BELLS of Saint James a few blocks away are calling the Episcopalians home to ponder their sins—serving red wine in the water glass, failing to replace a divot, neglecting to RSVP—when I drive up. Custalow is waiting on the front steps of the Prestwould. A couple of my older neighbors are making their way carefully down to street level. They seem amused. My neighbors and I don't exactly run in the same circles, but they don't judge.

Custalow drives while I try Sam McNish's number again.

This time, he answers.

I introduce myself, but more as an Oregon Hill boy than as a journalist. "Journalist" is not high on most people's popularity lists. I even evoke his old classmate, telling him Cindy Peroni says hello.

"You do know it's Sunday morning?"

Oh, yeah. Shit. It had not occurred to my heathen, still-asleep brain that Sam McNish does still have a ministry, in addition to his work with kids.

I apologize.

"You wouldn't have caught me," he says, "but I got one of the assistant pastors to do this morning's service. It's been a rough week."

I start to sympathize with him when he cuts me off.

"I know who you are, by the way," he says. "You work for that rag that did the hatchet job on me."

I guess it was foolish of me to think he would have forgotten. It's been three years since Mark Baer did that story.

He interviewed just about everybody within a block of Grace of God, the big old rambling house where Sam McNish tries to save the world. Some would say he dwelled excessively on the neighbors' complaints of noise, littering, and general rudeness. Some would say that the facts didn't back up their fears that crime was on the rise. Some would say that Baer didn't try hard enough to get both sides of the story. Some would say that his point of view was skewed by the fact that he himself lived a block away.

A lawsuit was threatened but never carried out. I think Sam McNish found out our lawyers were bigger than his. Baer was spoken to harshly about journalism ethics, if I may use an oxymoron. As is often the case, I would like to kick Baer's ass.

So you can't blame Sam McNish for holding a wee bit of a grudge against my employer, which continues its fine tradition, going clear back to antebellum days, of afflicting the afflicted.

I offer my apologies. I emphasize that I'm just another working stiff from the Hill, trying to earn a living. I mention, without lying, that I hold no affection for Mark Baer.

McNish carries on for a few minutes about my paper, going from his particular case to other injustices. I let him rave. Sometimes it's best to listen.

When he finally stops for two seconds to catch his breath, I jump in.

"Look," I tell him, "if you don't want to talk to me, fine. But I'm on your side."

I mention going out to the lake where they found Artesian Cole's body. I mention meeting the boy's mother and uncle out there, and how much I want somebody to suffer for this.

"I understand," McNish says, "that Mr. Cole created quite a scene down there at the newspaper. I guess I'm glad he didn't shoot anybody."

I note that the gun wasn't loaded and evoke such merriment as I can from my subject by describing the look on our publisher's face when she thought it was.

There is a slight thawing of the ice.

"I don't think any of us are going to get over this for a while," he says. "Artesian could have done great things with his life. Instead, this."

Things finally reach a temperature where I feel it's safe to ask McNish if it would be possible for me to stop by and talk with him, hinting that it would be good to give the public a more balanced picture of what Grace of God is about. I feel like an asshole, because I know that McNish, from my little chat with L.D. Jones, is a probable suspect in Artesian Cole's murder. The main purpose in my talking with him today is to get there before the cops jump him and he becomes a little less accessible.

Still, I tell myself I'm doing the Lord's work, just like Sam McNish. It's just that the deity I bow to is truth, and an afternoon with McNish might allow me to lay a burnt offering at that great god's feet.

We agree to meet at two thirty. I make a note to stop at two Bloody Marys.

McGonnigal and Peroni are waiting for us in a booth at the back of the Bamboo. They've been there twenty minutes, enough to get one drink up on Custalow and me.

"Rough night?" Andy asks with a grin.

I am noncommittal and order coffee.

The four of us grew up as friends, fighting and playing together. There were six of us then. Sammy Samms is gone from this Earth. Francis Xavier "Goat" Johnson is, against all possible odds, president of a small liberal arts college in Ohio and doesn't get back that often.

We were a somewhat odd group on the Hill, which was white as the columns on a Southern Baptist church. Custalow is a Mattaponi, although he prefers "Indian." I am, thanks to my long-lost daddy, one-half African American. We raised the social consciousness of more than one redneck with fists, bricks, and the occasional baseball bat. If they didn't embrace us, they feared our asses, which sometimes is just as good.

The conversation gets around to restaurants that provide a bigger, better space for smokers than nonsmokers. This being Virginia, there usually is a way to ply your nicotine habit while you dine, but often you are relegated to the back of the bus, shunted into some small side room where your fellow inhalers huddle in a cancer fog.

Since Peroni and I are both still slaves to tobacco, the conversation is not merely academic. We come up with three eateries that seem not to equate smoking with Ebola.

"But what do you do if the rest of your party doesn't smoke?" McGonnigal asks. "I mean, Tommy smokes, but he doesn't make me inhale that shit. He just goes outside."

Tommy is R.P.'s latest boyfriend. They are talking about tying the knot, now that they can do that in the state where they live and pay taxes.

"Yeah," Peroni says, turning to me. "Cindy doesn't let you take her to Camel City, I'm thinking."

"We have mutually agreed that we'll go for the nonsmoking."

This draws a laugh.

We talk about the Redskins, who suck, and about the University of Virginia basketball team, which shows no signs of sucking just yet.

"Just wait, though," Custalow says, "they'll wake up and figure they're U.Va. at some point."

It's part of the Virginia Way to expect the worst. A kind of good-natured cynicism covers the Old Dominion like a wet wool blanket. When exceptionalism pops up like a dandelion, we lop it off before it spreads.

Peroni brings up Artesian Cole and Sam McNish.

"That guy," he says, "he's high-hattin' us. Somebody said they saw him the other day, went up, and told him he'd been a year behind him in high school, and McNish acted like the guy was speaking Hindu. Just grunted something and kept walking."

"He always was odd," McGonnigal contributes. "He used to come to school with these sandwiches that had the crusts cut off. His mother would cut 'em off so little Sammy didn't have to eat anything but that good Merita white bread."

I note that this doesn't negate the fact that he's spent his adult life making no money and working seven days a week to help people.

"Well," Peroni says, "it still doesn't mean I have to like the son of a bitch."

Our conversation bounces from one talking point to another, sometimes without one damn thing to connect one point to the next. First thing you know, I look at my watch and it's two fifteen.

I get up to leave. The waitress must hate us. We hog one table for three hours and probably spent less than a hundred bucks.

"Come on," Peroni says, "it's only forty-five minutes to happy hour."

"They have happy hour on Sunday?" McGonnigal says, somehow surprised by this. "Aw, that ain't right."

I drop Custalow off and head out to learn what I can about the aforementioned Mr. McNish.

GRACE OF God looks a lot like the other houses on West Grace. The sign out front is about all that gives it away. The front porch needs a paint job and doesn't look quite level. It has not achieved the same level of gentrification as most of its neighbors.

I've learned enough from the files to know that McNish bought the place, probably for a song, back in the early nineties and started using it as a base for his ministry, helping people who needed a break any way he could. He founded Grace of God in 1995 but didn't get his after-school program going until four years ago.

In the 1990s, West Grace was kind of the poor side of the Fan, our Victorian neighborhood that starts around the Prestwould and Monroe Park and fans out until it ends, ten blocks wide by that point, at Boulevard.

Grace was more blue-collar than yuppie back then. Now, witness Baer's piece, there are many come-heres who wish McNish and his church would just go away. Hell, they'll probably use Artesian Cole's murder to restate their case about Grace of God being a crime magnet.

The doorbell is merely ornamental. I knock twice and wait. Finally Sam McNish appears.

He's apparently sparing with his smiles, not wishing to squander one on me. He's maybe five eleven, looks like he might weigh 140 pounds if he was wearing lead weights. He's got red hair that hasn't seen a comb lately and a scraggly-ass hipster beard. He has an earring in his left ear.

"Yeah," he says, "you must be the guy from the paper."

He turns and walks back into the house. I follow.

There's a big hallway leading back to what Kate would call a great room. The other rooms I pass along the way seem to have been converted into makeshift classrooms. There's a staircase leading no doubt to more rooms upstairs and another one going down to the basement. The place is huge.

The great room actually is pretty great, spreading across the back side of the place with a kitchen and dining room on one side and a living room on the other. Attached to the back is a big-ass deck. If the whole place weren't furnished with stuff Goodwill wouldn't take, it would be pretty impressive.

I note that this seems like a lot of house for one guy. I'm pretty sure McNish doesn't have a wife or live-in girlfriend.

"Well, it's a little more than just a house."

He flops down on an easy chair that doesn't look like it would stand much flopping. I opt for the beanbag, hoping I can get out of it later. Immediately one of the apparently large array of cats prowling the place attaches itself to me, no doubt sensing that I am allergic. I am convinced that cats aren't looking for affection so much as they are trying to find someone to annoy.

I ask him how this all got started. I pretty much know, but a little chitchat might make things go better.

He reaches over and turns on a tape recorder.

"I had a bad experience with the last reporter who came here," he says. "I'm pretty sure he misquoted me."

I don't like goddamn tape recorders. I don't use one, mainly because I went to the trouble to take a shorthand course thirty-two years ago. But I can't swear that I'll have every "a," "and" and "the" exactly the way my subject says them, and I don't want somebody coming back later and calling me on it if I use the wrong adjective. Hell, shorthand puts me ahead of most reporters. If you want a laugh, find some ballgame that several papers covered and go online the next day to check each sportswriter's version of the players' quotes. As Bootie Carmichael once told a managing editor after Bootie had badly mangled a player's quote after an ACC basketball tournament game, "I'm just trying to get the gist of what he said, Boss." Bootie always calls his superiors "Boss" when they ride his ass, because "Boss" spelled backward is doubleSOB, and that's two of 'em.

Since Bootie had left a "not" out of a quote about "taking Duke lightly," he had a pretty weak case.

I can get a quote right, but I'm not perfect. Still, I need this interview, so it's time to bend over and take it, tape recorder and all.

Once we get the damn ground rules straight, Sam McNish tells me his story.

He was still in Union Seminary, where he went after Princeton, when his mother died.

"She was pretty unhappy that I didn't go to law school," he says, "but she knew I was doing what I was called to do."

She left him more money than he expected. Her West End parents did not completely leave her out of their wills, maybe out of guilt, and she passed it on.

"I was almost finished at Union, and I already knew I wanted to do something other than preach on Sunday mornings, visit the sick, and fight the deacons over what color robes the choir should wear."

One day, walking around the city, he saw this big place on West Grace.

"I couldn't afford it today," he says, "but back then, places here were a steal, relatively speaking."

It took much of his inheritance, but he bought it, fixed it up, and started Grace of God. He's been here almost twenty years now.

"At first, the neighbors were OK with it. But then we got a bunch of people who came in with money and expected this place to be Mayberry."

It isn't exactly Mayberry now, and it damn sure wasn't back then. It was a block off Broad, giving the hookers easy access to the bus lines and their Fan clientele.

I still remember one City Council meeting a few years after Grace of God opened. The neighborhood was already trying to push the ladies and their pimps somewhere else by making West Grace semi-inaccessible.

An African American councilman who did not suffer fools or NIMBYs gladly asked one aggrieved homeowner, "Where do you think they go when you run 'em out of your neighborhood? Do you think they find Jesus?"

"Yeah," McNish says, doling out a small smile. "I remember that."

Things have progressed nicely enough, I think, to dispense with the off-speed stuff and bring the heat.

"So," I ask him, "why would somebody with a Princeton degree do this? I mean, you could be making real money."

He doesn't answer right away, like he's thinking about it. Maybe he hasn't had to explain his life recently.

"It was my fourth year at Princeton, early December," he says. "I was in a coffee shop right there on Nassau Street, right off campus. I was studying for some big exam, I don't even remember which one now. It isn't important. It wasn't important then. I just thought it was.

"I'd been up about twenty-four hours, and I was feeling a little froggy. Suddenly this beaten-down old man is standing right in front of me, actually blocking the light. He asked me for some spare change. I was pissed. I told him to get the hell out of there before I had him arrested, really went off on him for breaking my concentration. I'll never forget the look on his face when he walked away, like he was a dog you'd just kicked. I almost called him back. But I didn't."

McNish gets up and walks around, stopping to stroke the cat that has finally gotten the message and left me the hell alone.

"They found him the next day. He had crawled into an alley to get out of the wind, I guess, and he just froze to death there, not a block from where I blew him off."

McNish stops and looks not so much at me as through me.

"I might have saved him, maybe taken him to a shelter, given him one of my fine sweaters, even given him a place to stay for a night."

I'm thinking that plenty of people would have felt like shit after something like that, for about a day. Then must of us would have shaken it off, justified ourselves to ourselves somehow, and gone on our way.

Sam McNish obviously isn't wired that way though. More than a quarter of a century later, it's still bugging him.

"I'd gone to church, as a kid and even at Princeton. I'd studied other religions. But the whole idea that the homeless guy panhandling you or the abused kid on the corner is actually Jesus hadn't hit me before. When you turn your back, you're turning your back on Jesus."

He finished his time at Princeton, but from the day they found that bum's body, McNish apparently hasn't wavered from the path he set for himself. What he finally settled on, back in his hometown, was a church that offered something more tangible than pie-in-the-sky rewards, and that eventually evolved into the after-school tutoring that he and whoever else he can get to work for next to nothing are providing. They are getting by mostly on donations, although McNish does conduct actual services on Sundays and, I presume, passes the collection plate around.

I don't envy him. Saving the world is too much heavy lifting for me. Saving Willie is usually too much.

It's the wrong time to mention to McNish that I've never really bought in to the whole walking-on-water thing, although turning water into wine would be a nice trick. Even a hell-bound Christ-denier like myself, though, can spare a little admiration for somebody who gets up every morning determined to make the world a better place.

I've interviewed my share of bullshit artists posing as men of God over the years. Sam McNish doesn't feel like one of those.

I ask him about the last time he saw Artesian Cole.

"Last Monday," he says. "I was supposed to give him a ride home."

"What happened?"

"The car wouldn't start," he says. "I'm not too good with cars. I had it towed in the next day.

"At some point, while I was trying to get it started, Artesian said he'd just take the bus instead. He didn't want to wait. I'm sure he was afraid his mother would worry. And so he left, headed for the bus stop. And that was the last I saw of him."

The other kids in McNish's after-school tutoring program had all left by then. When I ask Sam if anyone else saw Artesian leave, he looks at me kind of strange.

"Why would you ask something like that?"

I don't answer.

The nickel drops.

"Oh," he says.

He doesn't say anything for what seems like a minute. I don't either.

"Probably not," he says at last. "He went out the side gate. He would have walked down Robinson and then over to Broad to catch the No. 6 bus. Maybe somebody saw him there."

I don't think so but don't say it. If somebody had seen the kid, L.D. Jones might not be asking the questions he's asking.

"Look," McNish says, "the police have already talked to me about this. They know what I know."

I don't bother telling the reverend that he probably will be talking to Richmond's finest again in the near future.

CHAPTER FOUR

Monday

I didn't get my interview with Sam McNish a minute too soon.

Custalow wakes me up before seven, something he knows not to do unless the place is on fire. I'm getting ready to head for the stairs, leaving my neighbors to fend for themselves, when my old friend informs me that things aren't quite that dire—unless you happen to be Sam McNish.

L.D. Jones, in his finest grandstanding form, has screwed me. He had to have known on Saturday that McNish's arrest was imminent. So he milked me for what he could get and then dropped the hammer as far from my deadline as possible. The early TV news, which normally leads with a story the video folk snatched off some website or are reading straight out of our paper, got the jump on this one. They have video of McNish, looking even scragglier than he did yesterday afternoon, being led out of Grace of God in handcuffs. The chief called the TV stations, obviously, but must have lost my phone number, the same one he called less than two days ago looking for information.

He has no comment for the masses, other than to say it's an "ongoing investigation," but the good-hair genius in front of the camera, like everyone else in Richmond who can read, knows that the late Artesian Cole attended McNish's tutoring sessions and was last seen there. Sarah got that into the follow-up story she did. The headline above the video reads, "Controversial minister arrested in boy's murder."

They even get a nice sound bite from one of the neighbors.

"I always thought there was something wrong over there," the guy in bathrobe and pajamas says. "You know, all those kids hanging around all the time and all."

And the TV guy tells us about all the complaints police have had about Grace of God over the years, mostly for excessive noise or trespassing. He fails to tell us that McNish has never been arrested for anything except for an act of civil disobedience, and that was in a failed effort to convince our idiot-in-chief that going to war in Iraq in 2003 was the perfect confluence of dumb and evil. If you disobey authority and you're right, shouldn't they expunge it from your record?

There's nothing to do about it except get up, get dressed, and turn an "off" day into an "on."

I call Peachy Love at police headquarters, something I've been told not to do. She calls me back ten minutes later. I can hear the wind whistling in the background and figure she's taking a smoke break so she won't be detected conspiring with a reporter. I appreciate that. Peachy will be job-hunting if L.D. Jones or anyone else in blue finds out that she still has connections with the ink-stained wretches.

"What the hell are you doing calling me at work?" is the way she greets her old friend.

I explain my situation. I can't figure out why the chief decided to pounce on Sam McNish in the middle of the night, less than two days after he'd indicated to me that he was taking a more subtle approach. Hell, this was about as subtle as a hand grenade.

"What I hear," Peachy says, lowering her voice so that I can barely make out what she's saying, "is that they got a hot tip from some volunteer or someone else who worked there. Like they were afraid the guy was gonna skip town."

"Yeah, I know about the volunteer."

I don't mention that the chief himself gave me that morsel, then told me I couldn't swallow it. Off the record, my ass.

"But whoever it was, she apparently called L.D. back yesterday and told him about the skipping-town part."

I tell her about my talk with McNish.

"He didn't seem like he was going to skip anything then. Hell, who would have fed all his damn cats?"

"Nevertheless, that's what I hear. Plus I hear there was drugs involved."

OK, maybe so. My nose is finely tuned to the scent of marijuana, if that's all we're talking about here. I did pick up a whiff of cannabis yesterday. God knows I've smelled enough of it growing up with Peggy. But, really, who gives a fuck? It'll probably be legal here in five years.

"And," Peachy goes on, "they seized his computer, so I'm sure they're going to town on it right now."

I want to know more, but Peachy says "shit," and hangs up, which probably means there was a cop or two coming her way on the street.

I give L.D. a call, too, just to thank him for hosing me. His secretary says she'll take a message. She sounds cheerful.

The newsroom, when I get there, is humming pretty good for a Monday morning. Word has gotten out about McNish's arrest.

Everybody's up in arms about the new health care plan our corporate masters have foisted off on us. It is, for about the thirtieth year in a row, shittier than the one the year before. This time, I think they want us to perform our own surgeries.

"It's the Virginia way," I hear Enos Jackson say to the kid intern who's working part-time on the copy desk. "We hated the plan we had last year, but this one makes us nostalgic for the good old days."

He starts softly singing "Carry Me Back to Old Virginny," our politically incorrect former state song.

The kid doesn't give a damn. He doesn't get health insurance and he doesn't need it.

We have a lot of kids these days. They work cheap with no benefits, and institutional memory's a luxury we just can't afford anymore, like bureaus, raises, and an editorial cartoonist. We have a neon "for sale" sign on our masthead, but nobody seems much interested in buying. And, from all I've heard elsewhere, we might be better off with the devil we know.

Wheelie spots me before I can get away. Mal Wheelwright, I realize as he comes closer, needs to get to the Y once in a while. All the stress of twenty-first-century print journalism makes some people lose weight. It seems to have had the opposite effect on our managing editor, who appears to have donut crumbs around his mouth.

"Thanks for coming in," he says. I appreciate that he knows this is one of my precious days off. "Did you know any of this was in the works?"

I tell him that a source let me know the cops were suspicious of McNish. I tell him that another source said he was considered a flight risk for some reason.

"Jesus, Willie. Does any of this ever get into the paper?"

I know Wheelie's upset. Nobody likes to get beaten on a hard news story by TV. It's like having a five-year-old whip your butt. I remind him, though, of my track record and the fact that nothing anyone told me made me think the police would act this fast.

"Yeah," Wheelie says, nodding his head. He seems to accept the fact that I have pulled his bacon from the fire a time or two. "Well, we need something strong for tomorrow."

I mention that I did have an exclusive interview with Sam McNish yesterday.

"Yesterday? Yesterday? Why didn't we have something in the paper this morning?"

Because, I explain, the interview was background for something I didn't see being a story for another day or two at least.

"Who knew McNish would be in jail this morning?"

Wheelie gives me the evil eye.

"I was hoping," he says, "that you would have."

That's just not right. I bite my tongue, though, and when he tells me he wants me to get Sarah Goodnight and see what we can "shake out of the tree" for tomorrow's editions (and, of course, our insatiable leech website), I don't object. I know Wheelie's getting heat from his corporate mistress, Rita Dominick. I tell him not to worry. He doesn't seem to be heeding my advice.

Sarah's poring over the eighty-six pages of six-point-type bullshit the representative of the new health plan gave us.

"Jeez, Willie. I don't think any of my doctors are on this plan."

"What do you need, besides a pediatrician?"

She gives me the finger.

We talk about how we are going to go about putting our newspaper where it should be, the lead dog in the chase for truth and justice. It isn't much fun getting scooped by TV. I mention the unnamed secretary or go-fer or whatever who seems sure Sam McNish is a bad man or at least wants the police to think so.

"I'll snoop around," Sarah says. "I know somebody who works there."

I give her Cindy Peroni's number and suggest that she might have some leads, too, having been a volunteer there for a while.

"Is that your squeeze?"

"Who wants to know?"

"Just askin'."

Richmond can be a really small town.

I tell Sarah that I'm going to see if I can get in touch with the man of the hour himself.

With a little help from my ex-wife and her ambulance-chasing partner, it could happen.

The secretary at what is now Green and Ellis says Ms. Ellis is busy but will call me right back, if I'd like to leave a message. I know "right back" could be hours that I don't have. I tell the secretary that Ms. Ellis's ex-husband says there's been a fire in the unit she's been renting him.

Hey, it could happen. It's an old building, and I try not to smoke indoors any more than is absolutely necessary.

Kate is on the phone in about ten seconds.

"What?" she says. "How bad is it? Did you call the insurance guy?"

I was kind of hoping she would ask me if I was OK. Considering that I've just lied like a dog to get her attention, though, I suppose I deserve to have my feelings hurt.

When I explain my little subterfuge, she seems unhappy.

"Bastard! You got me to ring off a call from a client for this?"

Kate seems a little stressed lately. Marcus Green has made her a partner to keep her from leaving. I know she's putting in some long hours and not getting rich doing it. Grace is now close to two years old, and I don't think my ex has ever really taken any serious child-rearing time off, although she does have some help. She and Mr. Ellis, who also is a lawyer and makes much better money than Kate does, have done something I never thought anyone I knew personally would do: They have hired an au pair. She's from Sweden, I think. I saw her once, and I hope Greg doesn't become too fond of little Gisella or whatever the hell her name is. She looked like a man could become very fond of her.

"Au, what a pair," was Andy Peroni's text to me the next day after he and I ran into the Ellis family and the help at a street festival a couple of months ago. I don't think he was talking about Kate and Greg.

When my ex left Bartley, Bowman and Bush for the less-lucrative offices of Marcus Green, she did it for all the right reasons. Marcus, who has been called an ambulance chaser (because he chases ambulances) and much, much worse, does occasionally find himself on the side of the angels. He says it's good publicity to win one for the little guy once in a while. It gets him some business from the big crooks, who have big checkbooks.

I'm calling Kate and, by extension, Marcus because Sam McNish is just the kind of no-hoper who piques Marcus's interest. He can be assured of seeing his bronze dome in our paper a few times if he decides he wants to be Sam McNish's lawyer. Marcus is not averse to publicity. His TV ad is a hoot. He's up there giving it his best pit-bull-from-the-'hood scowl, and some hired voice that sounds like Shaft with a hangover says, "When it's time to get mean, you better call Green."

"I heard McNish had been arrested," Kate says, once she has calmed down and realized there might be a good reason I've interrupted her busy workday. "Jeez. I've been reading about him for years. People are going to go batshit over this one."

Which is why, I tell her, that I'm sure Marcus Green will want to be standing in line at the city jail waiting to offer his services to this poor unfortunate.

"And maybe you can get a little face time with the suspect yourself," she says, ever the cynic.

I inform her that I've talked to Mr. McNish in the last forty-eight hours.

"I'm just trying to do a good deed in a naughty world."

She snorts.

"Marcus will be back here about one. Maybe you ought to come by and talk to us then."

I promise her I'll do that.

"Willie," she says, "that thing about a fire: You aren't smoking in my unit are you? If you are, I swear I'll throw you and Abe out on the street."

"Perish the thought."

"Which thought? That you'd smoke indoors or that I'd kick your ass out?"

I assure Kate that I am not ruining the resale value of her property. Being the honest sort, I cross my fingers when I say it. Hell, if I smoked indoors more than once every blue moon, she'd be able to smell it when she comes by, usually when she knows I'm not there. It isn't that my ex doesn't want to be around me. We've even had a nice day or two together since the split. She just likes to be able to snoop unimpeded.

I ask her if she'd like to take me to lunch. She says she's going to run home between twelve and one to spend a little quality time with her daughter.

So I use the two hours before my meeting with Green and Ellis to go over to Oregon Hill and check on my daughter and grandson.

I haven't been around small children in a while, or at least ones in which I have a vested interest. For much of Andi's young life, I was working at being a full-time fool, letting her mother and the guy who stepped in when I abandoned them do the heavy lifting. Some things can never be undone, but you have to try.

Andi has circles under her eyes. She says she has to be at work in a couple of hours, and she was just catching a catnap when I called. Suddenly, she starts crying.

"I want to do this," she says. "I want to keep working. I want to get my damn degree. I don't want to be a dependent of Quip or his family. But some days it's kind of rough."

Little William has been a bit colicky, and I gather Andi was up much of the night with him.

I do the only thing I can think to do that might be of help.

"Lie down," I tell her. "If the baby wakes up, I'll take care of him."

And she lets me. She stretches out on Peggy's moth-eaten couch with her feet in my lap and is asleep in about thirty seconds. Watching my grandson in his innocent slumber while my daughter catches the only rest she'll have for the next eight hours is a gift I never deserved.

On the way to the Green and Ellis office, I stop and buy a Powerball ticket. It's probably my best gambit for being able to ever take care of Andi and William financially.

I arrive about one thirty. The great man himself greets me. Marcus Green has added an earring to his general appearance of black fury, rectitude, and hipness. With his shiny, shaved head, he looks like an African American Mister Clean.

"So, you want me to do your work for you again?" Marcus asks.

I remind him of how lucky he is to be in my good graces. Some of his most attention-getting cases in the last few years emanated from me.

"Yeah, but how come I never make any money off of them? You act like I'm goddamn Ellis Island or something, and you keep bringing me your tired, your poor, your huddled masses, yearning to breathe free."

"Hell, you know you crave publicity even more than you do money. You'd rather be on TV than eat a Ruth's Chris steak."

He frowns the frown he saves for hostile witnesses, and then the weather changes in an instant, the way it does with Marcus, and he breaks out in that loud, booming laugh of his.

"Willie, I can never bullshit a bullshitter."

Kate, standing to one side, just shakes her head. She wondered often, when we shared sleeping space, why men seem to have to do this dance before they get down to business.

"It's like you're dogs," she said one time, "and you have to growl a little, sniff each other's butts first."

I told her it wasn't the first time I'd been called a dog, and that I'd sniff her butt if she liked.

I tell Marcus what I know about Sam McNish, and most of what I've learned from L.D. Jones and Peachy Love.

"He sounds like a pretty good suspect to me," Marcus says.

"Yeah, but all he's done his whole adult life is try to make the world a better place. I just can't see him molesting and murdering one of his kids."

"He wouldn't be the first holy man to succumb to the devil. Sometimes these guys are just trying to stave off their own personal Satan by doing good works."

I concede that I have little use for what I know of religion and emphasize that this should make my judgment of McNish more credible.

"I could be wrong, but there is nothing in Sam McNish's background that causes this to make sense."

Marcus sighs and says he'll pay a visit to McNish, if he's willing to see him.

"I don't know why I let you talk me into shit like this," he adds as he escorts me out.

I make it clear that I'd like to be there when and if that conversation occurs.

"Let me see him first," Green says. "You all can have your good-old-boy Oregon Hill reunion after I set something up. Don't worry. I'll drop your name."

Not the best of outcomes. I'd rather be there from the start, but I doubt Marcus will screw me any worse than our chief of police has. How did this turn into Fuck Willie Day?

AT THE office, I go into our electronic archives. I'd still like to go back to maybe 1985 and strangle the Internet in its infancy. At the same time, I would kill whoever decided giving news away free via computer made sense.

I must admit, though, some things about computer hell are an improvement. I can sit at my desk and access just about anything we've written in the last quarter century.

I remember Shorty Cole mentioning other kids going missing. I type in a few keywords and, after a couple of hours of hit-and-miss, I have come up with the names of four other black kids, all boys, from the late Artesian Cole's side of town who seem to have disappeared.

One of them, who was twelve at the time, went missing five years ago. Another one, a fourteen-year-old, vanished four years before that. If they or their bodies ever turned up, this information didn't make it into our electronic archives. The other two went back further. One was from 1999, the other from 1994, twenty years ago.

I check one other thing and confirm that McNish didn't get the after-school program going until 2010, a year after the fourth boy vanished. It could mean nothing. The cases could be unrelated. I'm having a hard time, though, accepting the fact that Sam McNish has been dispatching little black boys for more than two decades.

It is hard not to notice, however, that the first boy disappeared the same year McNish bought his house.

I WENT back to my desk to write my story. I have precious little new information, but I am free to report what I already knew but didn't put in print because I was working under the faulty belief that our chief of police could be trusted.

I write about the chief's private chat with me on Saturday, mentioning that an unnamed person at Grace of God had made some incriminating statements about McNish. I hold back, for now, on writing that there were four other unsolved disappearances of kids who fit Artesian Cole's general description over the past two decades.

I fully expect to get a call from the chief tomorrow. He'll be yelling at me for going back on my word while I'm yelling at him for shafting me. Then we'll hang up on each other, and the next time one of us needs to use the other one, we'll reconnect.

We both want justice, but both of us would like to keep our jobs. Sometimes, our methods are at cross-purposes.

CHAPTER FIVE

Tuesday

Sarah called me last night to tell me she had gotten in touch with the worker who gave the cops all the juicy tidbits about Sam McNish. She got a pretty good lead from Cindy, who still knew some of the volunteers and semipaid workers there. One of them told Cindy who it almost certainly was, and she told Sarah.

Her name is Stella Barnes. She's been a teacher's aide and administrative assistant at Grace of God for about eight years.

Sarah got her address, a place on the western edge of the city, and paid her a visit.

"She didn't really want to talk to me," Sarah said, "but when she realized we knew pretty much everything the police knew, she let me in."

Stella Barnes more or less corroborated what she had volunteered to the police, the same information that worked its way up to L.D. Jones and over to me.

She saw McNish coming out of one of the bathrooms one day last summer with the boy, Artesian Cole, in tow and looking kind of upset. She thought it was suspicious. And she knew that McNish had given the kid rides home on occasion.

"I don't know, though, Willie. She seemed kind of sketchy. And she must have had like eight cats there. I don't trust anybody with that many cats."

I observed that having that many cats might make you a little weird, but it doesn't make you a liar.

"Still, she did seem a little jumpy."

"Was she on the record?"

"Oh, yeah. She never asked not to be. It's funny, she said she and McNish were close at one time, but that he had kind of changed."

I noted that she probably could hang some kind of half-assed story just on those two allegations. She said she'd rather wait a day or two.

I reminded her that Wheelie's hot breath is on the back of our necks. He wants some red meat.

"Oh, Wheelie," she said. "He'll wait."

Ah, the confidence of youth.

"By the way," she said, before she hung up, "I liked your honey. She seemed nice. She kind of reminds me of my mom."

I could have gone all night without hearing that.

"So, do I remind you of your dad?"

"Ewww. That's really sick."

TODAY, MY first order of business is paying a visit to the boy's mother. I was able to get Shorty Cole's number from someone in HR who owes me a favor, and he put me in touch with his sister.

Shorty asks me if I know of any jobs. I tell him I'll check around. Andi's worked in about half the restaurants and bars

in town. Maybe she'll have a line on something. Shorty might
make a good bouncer, if they can get past that one unfortunate incident in our lobby last Friday. It'll keep him until he
either does or doesn't have to go to jail.

"Could use some Christmas money," Shorty says.

I promise I'll check and call him back.

A man answers at Laquinta's house. He doesn't seem that
thrilled to talk to me, even after I convince him I'm not a
damn bill collector. Journalists aren't much farther up the
totem pole, just above lawyers, as I'm fond of reminding
Marcus Green.

Finally, though, he lets me talk to Artesian's mother. She
tells me that the funeral is tomorrow, and the house is full of
relatives, some all the way from New Jersey.

I'm about to tell her that I'll call back in a couple of days.
The funeral has, as the kids say, gone viral. They've had to
move it to the Arthur Ashe Center, and several black ministers
are coming to bemoan the fate of young black men. My timing's not so great.

But she surprises me, the way people do.

"You can come over if you like," she says. "I'd like to talk
about Artesian, what a good boy he was."

She seems to be choking back tears. I'm feeling a little
lump myself.

I clear my throat and ask her if an hour or so from now
will be OK, and she hesitates for a couple of seconds and
then says it will be. I am sure that I will be about as welcome
as a fart in a phone booth by the mourning party. Maybe
being part African American will help. In the deck of race
cards, mine is probably a two of clubs.

Laquinta Cole and her two remaining children live down
the back side of Church Hill, where whites dared not tread

until the recent past. Everybody's so giddy about Richmond's "gentrification," but if you're the original settlers instead of the new Renovation Hardware/Williams-Sonoma gentry, I'm not sure the rising tide is lifting your ass off the bottom. It might not get you anything but higher property taxes.

The house is at the other end of Grace, the same street where I and my fellow journalists ply our trade. It's a different kind of Grace, though, and it's not like the Grace where Sam McNish has set up his Jesus shop.

Grace Street wanders through the wilds of our fair city, lost, found, then lost again. Like Richmond itself, it does not run in a straight and unbroken line.

When I was a young reporter, about all I knew of Grace Street was the section that went by the paper and the part near VCU, most specifically where it led to the Village Café and the bars where they hosed the floor down at two A.M. every day.

Covering night cops not once but twice in my checkered career, I eventually came to know Grace better than most.

It can be a tad hardscrabble, passing near some of the city's toniest addresses but not quite there, like a rich man's star-crossed cousin or a beauty queen's plain sister. It has its bright spots, though, and the city's history is laid out along its chopped-up route.

It does have its quirks. For one thing, it keeps disappearing.

It starts at Chimborazo Park, not far from where I'm going today, as East Grace. It wraps around the park, going past a historical marker commemorating a seventeenth-century Indian battle (the white folks got one band of Indians to help them wipe out another one). From all appearances, it is a good place to smoke dope and screw. There's cobblestone on the streets here, either due to preservation or neglect. There are potholes that could swallow a Smart car.

And then, a block farther west, it dead-ends to accommodate a kiddie park.

You'll find it again a little higher up on Church Hill, where you can look down Twenty-Ninth and see the Confederate memorial at Libby Hill Park. It goes past Saint John's Church—Patrick Henry, give me liberty and all that crap—and some of Richmond's oldest homes, overlooking the river and a couple of my favorite eating and drinking establishments.

It disappears again at the edge of Shockoe Valley, by the old religious retreat with its view of downtown on the other side of I-95.

It picks up again for one short block on the west side of the interstate, and then it gives way to Capitol Square. To find it again, you go around the capitol, where the government of a rebel country resided for four years, a country in which my future mother's people sought to keep my future father's people enslaved. History cuts pretty deep here, so we try to skip over the uncomfortable parts.

Past the capitol, Grace is resurrected at Ninth Street and heads west past a federal courthouse and some places where you can soak in some culture if you like that sort of thing. Grace has been prettied up quite a bit in the last thirty years. Even the part around the newspaper looks better than it used to while preserving at least a hint of its so-called eclectic nature. You can go to church at Centenary Methodist or take in the cross-dressing brunch at Godfrey's on a Sunday morning. If you time it right, you can do both.

Grace continues unbroken into the area where VCU is gradually eating the city, bulldozing the old bars and cheap-eats places of my youth. Then it becomes houses again, an outlier to the Fan that has come up in the world since Sam McNish bought his place for a song and made it into Grace of God.

It goes on westward, a block off Monument Avenue, where we memorialize Robert E. Lee, Jeb Stuart, Stonewall Jackson, and Arthur Ashe with no sense of irony.

Like Grace of God and its guiding light, they are all ours, for better or for worse.

LAQUINTA COLE's place is within eyesight of the kiddie park, in one of those truncated sections of Grace. There are so many cars near her house that I have to park two blocks away, on the other side of Broad.

I stub out my Camel and go up the front steps. When I walk in the unlocked, cracked-open front door, I get some looks, but there are so many people here that you could feed yourself on chicken, potato salad, and collards for two days before they figured out you weren't family or friend. And my dusky demeanor ("Not quite white," is the way I overheard one woman on the Hill describe me once when I was about ten years old) gets at least my little toe inside the door.

I'm halfway to the big table and the big women around it when my passage is blocked by a bronze battleship.

"Can I help you?" the man asks. It doesn't sound exactly like a question. I recognize his voice from the phone earlier.

I tell him I'm that reporter, the one who called. He does not seem impressed. With his log-size arms folded, he looks more like a bouncer than a mourner.

I know I've seen his big ass somewhere before. At about six five and way on the other side of three hundred pounds, he would stand out in a crowd. And if that didn't do it, the squinty, like-to-fuck-you-up eyes, graying beard, and a nose that has stopped a few ill-conceived punches would have finally cashed a check at my memory bank.

The light bulb goes on.

"Big Boy? Big Boy Sunday?"

"Yeah," he says. "Who wants to know?"

Franklin Sunday is about my age. I know because he played for Armstrong when I was a schoolboy flash, or thought I was. Even then nobody but the newspaper called him anything but Big Boy, for good reason. I still remember an end sweep we tried to run my senior year. The pulling guard wasn't much bigger than me, and when he turned the corner, with me right behind him, there was Big Boy, the right defensive end. He picked the guard up, literally lifted him off the ground, and flattened my ass by throwing him into me.

He looked down at us and asked, "What else you got?"

I know Big Boy from later dealings too. On the night cops beat, he was always on the periphery. You'd hear a rumor that he was behind some drug-deal-gone-bad shooting or the disappearance of somebody whose absence seemed to have been involuntary. He was the guy off in the background, always with two or three other bad characters flanking him, maybe leaning on a car no journalist could afford, watching the cops try to find somebody who saw the most recent East End shooting. (Almost nobody ever did.)

He did a couple of years in prison for second-degree manslaughter, probably that little because the victim was what the prosecutors call "NK," as in "needed killing." But that was a long time ago.

I have never actually introduced myself to the man, haven't really been in a position to do so until now.

My recollection about our high school football days doesn't get much more than a nod.

When I mentioned growing up in Oregon Hill, he does react a little more.

"No shit?" he says. "Man, I thought that place was white as rice."

He hesitates.

"No offense," he says, "I mean, you don't exactly look like the Caucasian persuasion."

"A little of this, a little of that," I tell him.

He nods.

"Listen," he says, lowering his voice, "this ain't exactly a good time, know what I mean? Maybe later."

I agree with him but tell him that Laquinta Cole had invited me over, said she wanted to talk about it.

He looks doubtful, but then Laquinta herself comes in from the overcrowded living room. She recognizes me from the park the other day and steps between me and Big Boy.

"It's OK," she tells him, putting a hand on his elbow. "I'm good. Just want to talk about it. Let somebody know Artesian was a good boy, that he didn't do nothing to bring this on."

Big Boy gives me a look that tells me I probably shouldn't do anything to further upset the grieving mother, then wanders off in the direction of a just-delivered bucket of KFC.

She leads me to a room that has only half a dozen people in it and asks them for some privacy.

I sense I'm better off just jumping right in.

"Tell me about Artesian."

She goes on for about twenty minutes, with no interruption from me. There's no mention of the boy's father, who I assume is long gone.

"He was always trying to look after me," she says. "'Momma,' he told me one time, 'I'm gonna take care of you. I'm gonna get you a big house, and you won't never have to work again.' He wasn't no more than seven when he said that."

She talks about how he tried to look after his little brother and sister. I guess that's them I saw wandering around from hug to hug, looking lost.

Laquinta takes a breath.

"They got that man that did it," she says. "That so-called man of God. I trusted him, he seemed so, I don't know, so good. Now I hope they fry him. But I bet they don't."

And I bet they'd better, if Sam McNish is guilty. In a city that's half African American and keeps score, anything else would not be well-received. I'm sure the commonwealth's attorney and L.D. Jones and everyone else can see "Ferguson, Missouri," written all over this one.

Then she says something that catches my ear.

"It's just like the other ones, and nobody got caught for them."

"The other ones?"

I'm mostly sure I know what she means, from the research I did earlier, but I want to hear her say it.

And she goes on to tell me about the last two boys who went missing.

"They just disappeared, like the ground swallowed them up," she says. "The police seemed like they weren't that interested. One of 'em told Patrice Fetterson that her boy had probably got mixed up with drugs and gangs and all. But that was bullshit, pardon my French. That boy was as good as gold, good as 'Tesian."

Neither of the boys seemed to have any connection to Sam McNish, although Mrs. Cole says at least one of them was involved in another after-school program, before Sam started his.

She shows me some of the medals and awards Artesian had won. It's my opinion that we as a country are suffering from award inflation. Cindy told me one of her nephews got a youth basketball trophy for being the most enthusiastic. He apparently never got to play much, but he yelled a lot. Still, Artesian Cole's trophies are impressive. He seems to have been the most valuable player on whatever kiddie team he was on, he had perfect attendance, and his grades seemed to range from A to A minus.

I promise his mother that I will work all of this into the story I've decided I'm going to do for tomorrow, the one they damn sure better make room for.

She thanks me for coming. I thank her for her time. There isn't much else to say without being an insincere asshole.

I mention the other two missing boys that showed up on my search, the ones who vanished back in the nineties.

"Hadn't heard about them," she says, shaking her head. "But you know, people disappear around here and it doesn't seem like it's that big a deal. It is to us, but not to nobody else."

I can't say much to that.

On the way out, I nod to Big Boy Sunday, who is standing in the yard talking to a couple of guys with tattooed necks.

He walks over.

"You gonna write something about Artesian?" he asks me.

I tell him that I'm headed to do that right now.

"Do right by him," he says. "By his momma too." He puts a slight pressure on my arm and gives me a look that is downright inspirational.

Looking back on the porch, I see the little girl, Artesian's sister, who must be all of five. She waves and I wave back.

BEFORE I can get started on the two stories I want to write, I get a call from my favorite police chief.

He confers a few choice names on me, as I figured he would. He accuses me of running information that was off the record. He's right, although I explain to him, as best I can between rants, that he forfeited that off-the-record crap when he burned me by arresting the guy, handing the story to the

TV guys, and leaving me sitting here with my thumb up my ass.

I tell him that, if he wants to complain to my boss, fire away. I can't be any deeper in the doghouse than I am now for holding off until the good-hair folks on the local network affiliates already had it.

"It was . . ."

"An ongoing investigation." I complete the tired excuse for him. "That's fine, L.D., but when you ask for my help and then want me to sit on what you tell me, I need a little love in return."

"Well," he says, "you haven't heard the last of this. And it'll be a cold day in hell before you get anything else from me."

I mention, as he is hanging up, that I hope he enjoys the story I'm writing for tomorrow's paper.

"I'd tell you more about it," I say, because I know he's still there, listening, "but it's an ongoing investigation."

CHAPTER SIX

Wednesday

This morning, our dwindling readership found out that Artesian Cole's murder might not have been a one-and-done, random act. Actually, a lot of them learned about it on the eleven o'clock news last night. Somebody coded the story wrong, and it was released as soon as the copy desk finished with it rather than being embargoed. Thus, our faithful reader, eating his cornflakes and reading what he already heard on TV last night, is asking his wife, "Tell me again why we subscribe to the paper?"

I don't have nearly enough information on the other four boys who've gone missing, going back twenty years, but I did manage to get up with relatives of two of the four.

"It's like our lives just stopped," was the way the mother of the first boy said. "There's not a day I don't think about him."

L.D. Jones, who probably lost some sleep over this one, has already released a statement, probably written by Peachy

Love. The police, the statement goes, take all crimes very seriously, and they never close the books until justice is done.

That was hardly the consensus of the eighty-six people who had already weighed in on our website by the time I had my first cup of coffee. The verdict there was: fire all the police and let God sort 'em out. If L.D. Jones were not African American himself, the rage level might have been a couple of notches higher. Plus, L.D. has only been the chief for seven years. He's made enough missteps on his own without having to inherit the past.

The story doesn't come right out and say that there's been a serial killer out there molesting and murdering young black boys for the past twenty years. We let the readers draw their own conclusions. All we do is insinuate.

Many of the online ranters have, in addition to calling for the dismantling of our police department, insisted that we execute Sam McNish as soon and as painfully as possible. Who needs trials? The people have spoken.

THIS PROMISES to be a busy day. In addition to the actual workday, starting at three or thereabouts, there's Artesian Cole's funeral. And assuming a mob hasn't stormed the jail and hauled him away to rough justice, I will be talking with McNish, in the company of his esteemed attorneys.

I knew Marcus couldn't keep his hands off this one.

I call Sarah at the paper before I leave for Artesian's funeral.

"You wouldn't believe the calls we're getting," she says.

I tell her that it's heartening to know that some of our readers still have vocal cords and do not communicate exclusively by tapping their fingers on keyboards.

"It wouldn't be so damn heartening if you had to listen to all this crap."

The black community tends to blame our paper for a variety of sins, many of which we are guilty. Although I personally was still in short pants when we urged white people to leave the city rather than integrate the schools, we do inherit the sins of editors past. Like L.D. Jones, we catch heat because we're the ones here to catch it.

Sarah is writing a story for tomorrow on what the other workers at Grace of God, and especially the ones involved with the Children of God program, think about all this. She tells me that there is a lot of sympathy for Sam McNish, but there are a couple of them who said he wasn't exactly an angel.

"Like what?"

"Well, the younger ones thought he was pretty cool, but some of the older ones, almost as old as you . . ."

"Watch it."

"They said sometimes they could smell beer on his breath when he came back from wherever he'd disappear to in the middle of the day, and one of them said she was pretty sure she smelled dope on him."

"What a shock."

"And there was this other thing, although I can't use it."

"What?"

"Well, one of the women told me, off the record, that she thought he might have had a thing going. With Stella Barnes."

"And Mr. Motive rears his ugly head."

Sarah sighs.

"So," she says, "you're going with the woman-scorned angle?"

"I'm not going with anything. I'm just trying to find some daylight here."

I tell her I'll see her after the funeral and after I meet with Sam McNish.

"Be sure and ask him if he's been hooking up with Stella Barnes."

"You think?"

THE FUNERAL services at the Ashe Center start at eleven. I get there at ten fifteen and the place is already packed. There must be three thousand people. I wind up sitting on the bleachers, about half a mile from all the ministers and choirs. At least I can get out quick if this thing runs long.

A couple of mourners recognize me and ask me when my paper is going to get off its ass and do something about all these black boys disappearing. I could say that what little is being done is being mostly done by me, but this is no time to get in an argument. This is a time to shut up and take it.

And God knows the service does run long. It's almost as long as the one they did for Arthur Ashe himself. I covered that one. I had no feeling in my butt for two days.

Four preachers, three choirs, and a handful of volunteers are there for the long haul. The crowd doesn't seem to mind it. I am amazed at how no one but me appears to be in the least bit of a hurry to get anywhere else. There is a certain grace in giving the departed's kin as much time as they need to validate their grief.

Sitting beside Laquinta Cole in the front row is a hulk that has to be Big Boy Sunday. He has his arm around her. The light finally penetrates my thick skull. Big Boy is Laquinta's man—front door, back door, whatever. I know he doesn't live with her. I've already checked on that, but he's definitely large and in charge.

"Lord," one of the preachers inveighs, "we know you have made room among your streets of gold, in one of its finest mansions, for Artesian Cole. We ask that you look kindly on his loving mother. And we ask you to help us understand, if not to forgive, the depraved human being who took Artesian from us, who lured him in with the promise of a better life and then betrayed him in the most heinous way possible. Give us the strength to forgive."

"Ain't enough muscle in the world for that," a man two seats down mutters, to a chorus of "amens."

The preacher might as well have said Sam McNish's name. I think this crowd has already rendered its verdict. My story on the four other boys has only turned the flame up higher.

I sneak out as gracefully as I can at twelve forty-five. On the way, I make eye contact with L.D. Jones, standing there by the exit door in full police regalia.

He says something to me. I can't read lips very well, but I think he said, "Bastard."

I MEET Kate and Marcus at the jail. He's dressed to the nines, even by Marcus's standards, and I realize he must have been at the funeral too.

Sam McNish looks like he's lost ten pounds he didn't need to lose and he definitely could use some sleep. He's been a guest of the city for three nights now. He's spent most of his adult life trying to help our future felons avoid places like this.

"So," Marcus says after a bare minimum of pleasantries, "did you do it?"

Despite the fact that he is wearing jail garb, McNish seems surprised that anyone would even ask such a question.

"Of course I didn't do it. You know that."

"I don't know it," Marcus says. "Nobody knows it. As a matter of fact, I just came back from a funeral where about three thousand people are cocksure that you did do it, that you've been messing with and killing young black boys for twenty years or more."

McNish seems to accept the fact that his innocence is more obvious to him than it is to the public.

"What can I do?" he says. "How can I prove I didn't do it? How can I prove a negative?"

Kate cuts in.

"You can start by walking us through that day."

He looks at me.

"I've already told him what happened. It's already been in the paper, hasn't it?"

"Well," Marcus says, "tell us again."

The bottom line, when he's done: He can't prove he didn't kill Artesian Cole.

"But not to worry," Marcus tells him. "We don't have to prove you didn't do it. They have to prove you did."

"I never would hurt any of my students. Never. I loved Artesian."

It is suggested that, as pure as his thoughts are, McNish might not want to use that word to describe his feelings for a ten-year-old boy he's suspected of murdering.

He shakes his head.

"This is a sick world," he says.

"I hear that," Marcus tells him.

I cut in and ask McNish about Stella Barnes.

"She has some kind of incriminating things to say about you."

I mention the bathroom incident and the rides home.

"Of course I took him home. I was going to the day he . . . the day he died. And the bathroom thing. Good lord, she must be talking about the time Artesian had an accident. He is—he was—a smart kid, but he had this kind of, uh, bladder problem. He wet his pants. He was embarrassed. I helped him clean up and told him it was OK, that he was OK."

He looks around at the three of us.

"Is this what this is all about? Coming out of the bathroom with the boy? Giving him rides home?"

I ask him the question this has all been leading up to.

"Were you, uh, seeing this Barnes woman? Because I heard you were."

I can feel Kate's eyes boring a hole in the back of my head. She hates surprises.

He is quiet for a moment.

"Yeah," he says finally. "We spent some time together."

"But not anymore?"

"She's a nice lady. But I think she thought there was some future in us, and there wasn't."

"Why not?" Kate asks.

He looks her in the eye.

"I am married," he says. "I am married to my church and its mission. I don't think Stella could get her mind around that."

"Well," I say, "from what I heard, you found time to spend a few nights at her place, married to the church or not."

He drops his head.

"I was weak," he says.

No, I want to say, you were human.

"Do you think she went to the cops out of spite?" I ask him.

He shakes his head.

"No, I can't believe she'd do that. She was hurt when I told her we shouldn't go on seeing each other, but she's not a spiteful person."

When I mention that Ms. Barnes told the police she was afraid he might skip town, he seems completely befuddled.

"There is another thing," Marcus says. "I have it on good authority that they found some dope at your place. And that they found porn on your computer."

Now it's my turn to be surprised. Marcus actually has a source in the police department I don't know about.

McNish doesn't seem surprised.

"They probably found about half an ounce of marijuana," he says. "I like to take a toke now and then. Is that a crime?"

Well, yeah it is, I tell him, unless we've been colonized by Colorado.

I mention the beer some of his more prudish staffers have noticed on his breath.

"I go over to the Village sometimes for lunch," he says. "And yes, sometimes I have a beer."

"And the porn?" Kate asks.

He shakes his head.

"Like just about every other adult human being, I have looked at porn. But I can assure you that there is nothing on there involving children."

He puts his head in his hands.

"But they'll put all this stuff together, and it will be the end of Grace of God. All our donors will drop us. Then what's going to happen to all those kids?"

Marcus correctly points out that we need to focus on saving Sam McNish's ass first and then worry about his church.

He does not seem comforted by this.

Marcus tells him to buck up, that he's in good hands.

"Are they treating you well?" he asks.

"Oh, sure. Two of my former students and a couple of kids' family members are in here. They kind of look after me, protect me from the ones that don't know me."

From the ones, he means, who think he's a child molester and murderer and would like to give him a little turnabout.

We leave him with promises we might not be able to keep. Kate and Marcus are committed now; he's their client. Me, I'm a nosy bastard, to use L.D. Jones's word, who doesn't believe anything until he's seen some proof.

I GET some good news from Andi when I call. Somebody at one of the places in the Bottom is going to hire Shorty. Andi worked at the place for a while, but it was too rough. She has seen a few beer bottles broken over a few heads, but this place did not meet her standards.

"They could use a little muscle," she tells me. "A lot of muscle, actually. The last security guy they hired got beat up in the parking lot after work last week by a couple of guys he bounced."

Well, guys who hold the publisher hostage in the lobby can't be choosers. This is a paying job. It even has a few benefits. Considering the last security guy's plight, I guess benefits are a good thing.

She gives me the manager's number. I call Shorty. He answers and I pass the information along to him.

"That's a rough place," he says, then remembers his manners. "But thank you, man. I appreciate it."

I tell him I appreciate him not shooting our publisher. I more or less mean it. Whoever follows Rita Dominick will be more of the same, so what the fuck?

"Aw, man," Shorty says. "The thing wasn't even loaded,"

It is always good to do your fellow man a good deed, especially when you don't have to knock your ass out beyond making a phone call to do it. Look to your laurels, Mother Teresa.

LUNCH, TWO Millers, and a couple of Camels later, I'm at the office. I feel like I've already done a day's work, and I'm just punching in. When I was twenty-five, I could do this shit standing on my head. Now I'm just wishing for a peaceful, crime-free evening, although experience has taught me that, the more I need a night like that, the less likely I am to get it. I will never forget that god-awful New Year's Day a decade or so ago when I drew the short straw and had to work the holiday, back before I was sentenced to my second term as full-time night cops guy. I wasn't hung over, because you have to sober up first for that, but I had slept two hours and was praying for a quiet, short shift.

Instead, it was one of the saddest days in our city's oft-troubled history. A whole family—mom, dad and their two young daughters—was slaughtered in their home on the first day of the year by a couple of ex-cons who had no reason to do what they did other than pure, damn evil. I remember throwing up in the shrubbery after visiting the scene, sick on something other than booze for a change. That's what you get when you wish for a quiet day.

This one promises to be true to form. There's an e-mail from the lovely Ms. Dominick. "See me," it says. She is as parsimonious with words as she is with raises.

I assume she means at her place, not mine, so I take the elevator up to suit land. Sandy McCool, our longtime administrative aide, tells me the publisher is on the phone but should be off soon.

I ask Sandy how it's going. We've known each other a long time, and I know she's about the only person on this particular floor who won't bullshit me.

Sandy just rolls her eyes and tells me not to ask.

Uh-oh. That's a little worrisome. We haven't done layoffs for a while. I know the suits miss that. Like sharks, they get turned on by blood in the water. What they do mostly now is through attrition. I imagine the folks up here, when they meet at the Commonwealth Club after work for bourbon-and-waters, do high-fives every time a veteran employee who has had the nerve to build up to a pretty good salary over the decades retires or takes a PR job. Or, better yet, dies.

Soon Ms. Dominick is off the phone, and I am summoned in.

"Wheelie told me you sat on some of this stuff about the Cole boy," she says by way of greeting.

Thanks Wheelie. When confronted by our tiger shark of a temporary publisher, he probably panicked and nudged me off the boat as chum. I don't really blame him though. Wheelie's caught in the middle.

Fine, I tell her. And how are you?

"Cut the crap," she says, doing her best imitation of some cigar-chomping newspaper publisher in a 1930s movie, sans the cigar. "I know you know a hell of a lot more than what you choose to share with our audience. I just want you to know that this has got to stop. If I ever hear about you holding back information again, you're done."

"When I have a story, it will be in the paper," I tell her. "When a source tells me it's off the record, I'll honor that source, unless he burns me."

I am somewhat emboldened by the knowledge that, like winter and bad haircuts, Rita Dominick won't be with us forever. She's just marking time until the real suits sell our asses down the river to some chain that will make us yearn for the good old days. Right now, we're only enduring the death of a thousand budget cuts instead of an ISIS-worthy beheading.

I wish the publisher a nice day and walk out, rather rudely I guess, because she seems to have something else to say. Fuck it, I can always get one of those state jobs where you use a lifetime of truth-gathering skills to hide the truth.

I don't think she'll fire me. I'm not all that expensive, and who else is going to do this crap? It would be good, though, if I were to produce something that could serve as a Band-Aid on the massive hemorrhage that afflicts our print circulation. That might get Rita Dominick off my back for a few days at least.

CHAPTER SEVEN

Thursday

Sarah has a story in today's paper on the other Grace of God workers, with a special focus on Stella Barnes. The picture they paint of Sam McNish is hardly flattering, but it doesn't exactly scream "serial killer" either. Yeah, he's been known to have a beer or two at lunch. They did find some porn on his computer, but it wasn't of the felonious type. I got Peachy Love to give the names of a couple of the sites. Hell, I recognized them. I used to worry about Kate catching me occasionally taking a peek, until I caught her doing the same thing one day.

"I just wanted to see what all the fuss was about," she said.

Yeah, I told her. Me too.

The general consensus in Sarah's story, though, is that McNish is a good man who has a few minor vices. And the black parents who talked about the ministry had almost nothing but good things to say about Grace of God. There were a couple who said McNish might have been a little too affectionate, looking back on it, but that was about it.

I've arranged a meeting myself with Ms. Barnes this afternoon. Yeah, I know Sarah has talked to her already, but I'll risk hurting her feelings to get my own personal read. I got Cindy to intercede for me, but Stella Barnes might have said yes anyhow. She seems, unlike most Americans, amenable to talking to the press.

My story today is your basic kid's funeral tearjerker.

Don't get me wrong. There are some stories for which tears are the logical response, and this is surely one of them. I put a few grafs in about the crowd at the Ashe Center being somewhat worked up over the fact that Artesian Cole seems to be the fifth young black male to have disappeared without a trace in the last twenty years or so. Unlike the aforementioned parents, they mostly have no residue of goodwill for a white man suspected of killing African American kids. I note that there is nothing to link these other boys to Grace of God or Sam McNish.

It is never a good idea, in my opinion, to look at the comments that trail your story on the website like toilet paper stuck to your shoe.

"Did you read that shit?" Sarah asks me.

I tell her that I didn't, not wanting to encourage her. Reading the kind of opinions that turn up on our site, especially with a story as close to the bone as this one, will make you want to write the human race out of your will.

But I couldn't help myself. I guess it's like porn. You know you shouldn't look, but something pulls you in, and before you know it, you're forty-five minutes into living, breathing proof that human beings are a malignancy on our planet. If there is a God, I find myself thinking, why the hell are we still here? Isn't it about time for another flood?

The yappers are more or less divided into two equally reprehensible groups, both earnestly involved in their life's work:

judging and affixing blame while assiduously eschewing spell check.

First, there is the Kill the Preacher party.

Hang him! Hippacrit! Burn him alive!

Man of God, my ass. They out to nail him to a cross. Do to him what he done to that boy!!

I knew that fagot was up to no good.

And then there is the Blame Momma contingent, for which there should be an especially toasty little corner of hell reserved:

What kind of woman would leave her son alone with a animal like that?

Those people are never going to get there act together until they learn good parenting.

Fat welfair bitch. I bet she was pimping him out.

We do have some standards, believe it or not. By the time I go online again an hour later, our masters of the ether have taken the comments down.

I have time to kill before I interview Stella Barnes. So, it being two weeks before Christmas, I do something that's almost as pleasurable as sticking needles in my eyeballs. I go to the mall.

I'm a city guy. If the Thalhimer's and Miller & Rhoads department stores were still downtown, I might never cross the line into the county. But of course they're long gone, the buildings given over to the arts and urban housing, so the man looking for gifts for his mother, daughter, grandson, and sweetie must sometimes bite the damn bullet.

Everybody out here seems to be driving the kind of vehicles you'd want if you were dodging IEDs in Afghanistan. I can't see the stoplights because the boat in front of me is so big it's blocking out the sun. When I finally make it into the mall's county-size parking lot, I'm a taxi ride away from most of the stores where I think adequate yuletide bounty might be purchased. Why can't I just get everybody gift certificates, I asked Cindy. She didn't say anything, just gave me The Look.

Loaded with sizes and suggestions, I venture through the gates of hell into the mall itself. This is one of the newer ones, with a plaza or some such shit in the middle so that, if you are brain-damaged or very easily led, you can pretend you're in a real town, where real stores line the streets and everybody doesn't have to go to the goddamn mall to shop.

How do you know the mall isn't a real town? Well, if you're a reporter, try doing a man-on-the-street piece there: *Do you believe the economy's getting better? What do you think of the Kardashians?* That sort of shit. Before long, mall security will come up and escort you and the photographer outside, because it isn't a public street. It's a fucking mall, which seems to be like the Vatican, a little city-state that makes its own rules. You have to ask permission to talk to the happy shoppers.

I manage to buy a grand total of three gifts before my interview. Two of them might not be the right things at all, seeing as how sadists make up women's clothing sizes so that no man is ever exactly sure what he's got. My only bright moment is when the girl in Victoria's Secret asks me if I'd like them to gift-wrap the lust-inducing underwear I'm hoping Cindy will like, or at least model for me.

No, thanks, I tell her. I'll just wear them.

On the way out, I see a familiar face. Three of them to be exact. Philomena Slade has her great-nephews in tow. Jamal and Jeroy, Chanelle's twins, seem to be on a pre-Christmas high. Momma Phil, my first cousin once removed, looks exhausted as the boys romp around her. They seem to be in constant danger of knocking over the various seasonal crap the mall has put up, if not some hapless patron.

"If you all don't behave," Philomena says after she greets me, "there ain't going to be any Christmas."

The threat is toothless. The boys must be eight years old by now. They're growing up on the side of town where Santa Claus, the Easter bunny, and the tooth fairy don't last past the first grade. But they calm down a little anyhow. Their great-auntie still has some sway over them, even if they look like they're only about two years from being as tall as she is.

We talk about the topic that's on everyone's mind, especially in the black community.

"That was awful about that Cole boy," Philomena says. "He was two grades ahead of the twins in school. They said they didn't know him, but all the kids spoke well of him. I'm so glad Jamal and Jeroy didn't get involved in that mess. It just tears your heart out."

It hadn't occurred to me that my kin by my very late father were considering sending their kids to Sam McNish's program.

"I was thinking about it. Chanelle didn't want any part of it. I was the one pushing it. Shows how much I know."

She stops long enough to reel in the boys, who seem ready to jump one of Santa's elves.

"I see you're writing about it for the paper," she says. "Do you think that McNish fella did this?"

I tell her I have no idea, but that I'm hoping to learn more about it this afternoon.

Nobody at the paper, myself included, has done much in terms of interviewing people in the East End about the disappearances. We got in touch with a couple of the parents whose children have disappeared over the last twenty years, but that's about it.

I ask Philomena why someone didn't say something about these kids going missing over the years.

"It isn't like it happened in a year or two," she says. "I'm not sure those four—five with the Cole boy—are all there is, either."

"There might be more?"

Momma Phil sighs and chooses her words carefully. She is a thorough, patient woman, the kind of woman who waited twenty-eight years to see her son finally absolved of a crime he didn't commit.

"I don't want to get you all chasing your tails about this," she says finally, "but there has been stories for almost as long as I can remember. The kids would come home and tell their folks about some man, some white man, that would be hanging around, maybe offering somebody a ride, or in some alleyway. They even had a name for him. Frosty."

"Because he was white?"

"Yeah."

"But he wasn't ever caught or anything?"

Philomena shakes her head.

"I'm sure not. I don't even know if he was real. Most of us kind of thought the kids were making it up, the way kids do. But they still tell that story. I know I've heard some parents try to scare their kids with it, like 'If you don't straighten up and fly right, Frosty gonna get you.'"

She says she's sure people mentioned it to the police "but that didn't go anywhere."

I suggest that she might ought to threaten to sic Frosty on Jamal and Jeroy.

Philomena snorts.

"Frosty would be begging for mercy. Ain't nothin' scares those two."

She takes her leave. The boys seem bent on throwing each other into the fountain nearest us.

On the way out to talk with Stella Barnes, I mull over
Momma Phil's little bombshell. How have we gotten so out of
touch with our readers? Nobody, in all the ranting about Sam
McNish and all those missing kids, ever mentioned "Frosty,"
or at least not in my earshot.

I call Sarah and ask her. She's never heard anyone she's
interviewed mention that name either.

I FIND the Barnes residence with the help of a city map. It's
a brick rancher on one of the segments of Grace Street out
beyond Libbie, almost all the way to the Henrico County line.
There are pines around the house and a few oaks. Nobody has
done much if any raking this fall, and the roof is missing a
few shingles. I know Ms. Barnes is divorced, and it doesn't
look like she's much into yard work.

I knock twice and think she's stiffed me, but then I hear
someone pushing back a deadbolt, and the door opens.

"I'm sorry," she says. "The neighborhood's gone down a
little. I've got to be careful."

Maybe not that careful, I'm thinking. Looks like a decent
suburban street to me, if a little on the geriatric side. I'm
guessing the house I'm in was built in the sixties. It's a hell of
a lot more substantial than any of the places we lived in on
the Hill, that's for damn sure.

Stella Barnes is forty-six, according to what Cindy found
out. She looks like she tried to give Father Time the slip about
ten years ago, with only middling results. The blond hair has
had some help, and I'm not sure her boobs haven't as well. The
last person I saw with this much makeup and eye shadow was
a cross-dresser. And her skirt is a wee bit short for a slightly
overweight lady of a certain age on a Thursday afternoon. I'm
struggling to keep my eyes above shoulder level. Don't look,

my big brain tells me. Do not look. Focus on the picture of Jesus, as blond as Ms. Barnes, hanging over the couch.

Over coffee, I get through the pleasantries and ask her about Sam McNish.

She goes on a bit about what a blessing "Sam" was to the city, using the past tense. But she manages to work in a few caveats.

"He did like to have a drink now and then," she says, "and I don't like to tell tales, but they said he used drugs."

I assume she's saying he smoked marijuana.

"But I don't think he used it around the kids. I certainly hope not."

We walk through what she's told the cops and Sarah already, but I want to hear it for myself, and she seems happy enough to oblige. When she uncrosses and recrosses her legs, I focus on Jesus.

She "isn't sure" if anything happened on the day she saw McNish coming out of the bathroom with Artesian Cole. She makes reference to thinking Sam "isn't like that," but says she felt it was her duty to tell the police everything she knows.

"It's like with those priests," she says. "They did all those bad things for years, and nobody stopped them."

When I have the story, pretty much the same way she told it before, I get to the part of the interview where sometimes the subject tells you to get the hell out before she calls the cops.

"I have heard," I begin, "that you might have been romantically involved with Sam McNish at one time."

She sets her cup down, and I think that I'm about to get my eviction notice.

"No," she says after a pause. "I mean, we might have had lunch or dinner a time or two, but we were just friends. To tell you the truth, I never saw him in a romantic way."

Maybe so, but that's not the way Cindy's friend who was still working there as of last week saw it, and McNish has already more or less admitted to sleeping with her. It has been my experience that phrases like "in all honesty" or "frankly" or "to tell you the truth" can be code for "I'm about to tell a whopper."

I ask her why she told the police that McNish might be a threat to skip town before he was arrested.

"I don't know," she said. "He just seemed a little jumpy, you know. And if he did what they think he did, wouldn't he run for it?"

We chat for another ten minutes or so, with Ms. Barnes going on about what a crime-ridden city Richmond is (murders and most other felonies are way down) and how it's dying (the population's been up every year since the turn of the century). I just nod my head. Unlike Sam McNish, I've never been one for trying to convert nonbelievers.

On the way out, she says she hopes to see me again. She gives my hand a little squeeze as I start backing away.

I hear the deadbolt click as I make my way to my Honda, where a pack of Camels is calling my name.

ON THE way in, I get a call. It's Kate.

"They had to put him in protective custody," she says, cutting to the chase.

Yeah, even guys in jail don't like child-molesting murderers. Could've seen that one coming, even if McNish did think the inmates who knew him had his back. L.D. should have put him in solitary when he first went in.

I ask Kate if she thinks we (meaning I) could talk with our favorite man of God again soon.

"Marcus and I are talking to him tomorrow, but I don't know if he'd be willing to have a reporter there too."

I remind her that I've already talked to him twice, once with them and once, when McNish was a free man, without them. When I tell her about my conversation with Stella Barnes, she says she'll see what she can do.

"If I'm going to share information with you, I expect some cooperation," I tell her, further reminding her that I'm the one who got Marcus Green and her involved in this case to begin with.

I hear a snort.

"You share what you want to share."

We're talking as much about dead marriages as we are about the present situation.

"Let me speak to Marcus," she says.

"Hell, you're supposed to be his damn partner, not his secretary."

A pause.

"OK. OK. Be at the office at noon. Don't be late."

That's more like it.

CHAPTER EIGHT

Friday

I meet Kate and Marcus at their offices at noon, as directed, after a late, pork-free breakfast at Perly's.

"So you think this Barnes woman had a little issue with my—with our client?" Marcus says as we head out the door.

He already knows that there was a little horizontal tango between them. Not much I can add, but I tell him that I really want to ask McNish a few questions I didn't think of the other day.

I tell him anything's possible, but I'd like to hear McNish's side of the story at least.

Jails, like nature, abhor a vacuum. Even though the serious crime rate in our city is down, the local hoosegow is still overcrowded. It's always easy enough to catch some knuckle-head with an ounce of pot or a small amount of some other illegal substance, and all those cops and courts have to have something to do. Otherwise, the politicians, always eager to please the citizenry by cutting taxes, might start trimming the law-enforcement fat.

So the lockup is more or less busting at the seams. I'm glad, as we make our way to the interview room, that they have separated McNish from his fellow inmates, some of whom are a tad rude. Assuming, of course, that he didn't rape and murder a kid or five, in which case, fuck him.

Most middle-class white guys who've spent the workweek in jail look a little worse for the wear. McNish doesn't. I mean, he didn't look all that spiffy when I interviewed him last week, so maybe he only had so far to sink, but he looks, well, at peace—not an easy thing to do for a guy who has just been separated from his compatriots in order to keep them from killing him.

His main concern seems to be that the jail isn't exactly knocking itself out to give him something a vegan can eat. As Andi would say, *Quelle surprise*. From what I've heard about the food here, he's lucky his protein isn't still moving.

Marcus asks McNish about Stella Barnes.

"I've already told you everything I know," he says. "She was a good worker who I saw a couple of times socially. She wouldn't have had any kind of grudge against me."

I contribute that it doesn't exactly look that way to me.

"What do you mean?"

I recount the high points of my visit with Ms. Barnes today.

"Passive aggressive isn't exactly my area of expertise," I tell him, "but there was a lot of 'he's a great guy, but . . .' out there today."

"You shouldn't have bothered her."

Kate cuts in.

"He's trying to save your life, for Christ's sake."

McNish gives the slightest hint of a smile.

"My life already is saved, for Christ's sake."

Kate, Marcus, and I all look at one another. Is this guy, I want to ask, for fucking real?

"Look," Marcus says, "we're not here to worry about your immortal soul, but think how much harm can be done down here on planet Earth if your Children of God thing gets bull-dozed, which I guarantee you is about to happen if we don't prove you're not a monster who kills kids."

McNish frowns.

"I just can't believe all this," he says. "I've already told you, and told the police, what happened that day. There's nothing else to say."

"Somebody must have seen that kid somewhere before he got snatched," Kate says. "He didn't just disappear."

Maybe, but I'm thinking that it's not that far from Grace of God to the bus stop, and the boy might have only gone a block before somebody grabbed him. Still, it does look like he would have made some noise when he was being kidnapped.

Kate is going to haunt Artesian's route from McNish's place to the bus stop on Broad, in hopes of finding someone who saw something, anything. We assumed L.D. Jones's min-ions are doing the same, but L.D. has a tendency, once he has the most likely suspect behind bars, to go a little light on alternative theories. It is not one of his better qualities.

As we're leaving, McNish makes a strange request.

"I want to talk to him," he says, pointing at yours truly.

"Hell," Marcus says, "he's not even a lawyer."

McNish nods his head.

"Exactly. No offense."

So Marcus and Kate leave me alone with the inmate. The look Kate gives me says, plain as spoken English, that I'd better not be holding out.

I'm wondering, why me? McNish answers without my having to ask.

"You didn't run any of that stuff from our interview until they'd already arrested me. You seem trustworthy, as journal-ists go."

Yep. I'm a tall midget.

"Plus," he says, "you're from the Hill. And maybe I can save your soul."

Well, I haven't heard that one in a while. Most people gave up on my soul a long time ago.

"We'd better worry about saving your ass right now," I remind him. It strikes me as funny that a guy who dropped Oregon Hill like bad meat a long time ago would put any stock in our shared provenance.

"So," I ask. "What's on your mind?"

It takes him a few seconds to answer.

"Most of the people who were helping me at Children of God have left," he says. "Maybe they've lost faith in me. It doesn't matter what happens to me, but the church matters. I want you to help me get that faith back."

How in the hell, I ask him, am I supposed to do that.

"I know you," he says, "or at least I know what you do. Lawyers are good, but you've got a reputation for knocking down doors, getting to the bottom of things, so to speak."

I tell him that I think he's overselling me a bit. A couple of lucky breaks on stories don't make me Sam Spade.

"Look," McNish says, "I know I'm in some deep stuff here. I guess Stella Barnes was a little more upset than I imagined about my putting some distance between us, and she does have a tendency to read drama into situations where there really isn't any. But somewhere out there, there's got to be an answer. I don't mind so much the wheel stopping on my number, but there's the church."

He stands up. The guard looks our way.

"And there's another thing. Whoever did this might do it again, don't you think?"

Well, yeah, that's a good reason to do a little digging.

We talk awhile longer, drifting to our mutual acquaintance, Cindy Peroni.

As I'm leaving, he calls my name.

"Willie," he says, "I'll pray for you."

Normally it sets my teeth on edge when people say that. It implies a moral superiority. Granted, my moral superiors are legion, but nobody likes to have his nose rubbed in it.

With McNish, though, it somehow doesn't grate. Maybe because, no matter how much of a waste of time prayer is, McNish seems to mean it. A man who is on the cusp of being sent to either the death chamber or something worse appears to be worried about me. It's kind of touching, in a weird kind of way.

When I check my messages, there's one from Big Boy Sunday.

"We got to talk."

I call back.

I am greeted with "What?" Big Boy is obviously a little weak on his phone manners.

"Oh, yeah," he says when I identify myself. "I wanted to thank you for gettin' Shorty on the payroll again. You must of pulled some strings."

Not many, I tell him. I note that the woman he seemed bent on shooting probably was going to be shot by somebody eventually anyway.

He seems to think this is funny.

"Yeah," he says, "there's some that just needs shooting."

He tells me to meet him at an address about a block east of the Magpie, over in a part of town that's about ten years behind West Grace on the gentrification train.

He's sitting in the backseat of his big-ass SUV when I get there. Two young brothers trying to look tough are up front.

They don't frisk me, which probably speaks to the general perception that journalists are harmless away from the keyboard. One of them does jump out of the front and open the door for me. His scowl tells me this was not voluntary.

Big Boy is munching on a barbecue sandwich from Hawk's, which is making my stomach growl. He's holding the sandwich in one hand and has an order of fries in his lap that looks so greasy it might eat a hole through the container. A movie concessions-size soda is squeezed into the cup holder. My kind of lunch. A little of the sauce has dripped on the Don Ho shirt that serves as a tablecloth for his upper body.

"I appreciate your coming over here," he says.

I wait for him to get to it. He finishes off the 'cue in an amazingly short amount of time. He licks his fingers and inhales a couple of fries. Then he turns his attention to me.

"This fella, this McNabb, McNish, whatever, is he going to take the rap for killing the boy?"

"Unless they can come up with somebody that looks more guilty. He's sure the leader in the clubhouse right now."

"Don't get me wrong," Big Boy says. "I want justice here. That boy, he was like a son to me."

Big Boy and Laquinta Cole have been together for most of Artesian's life.

"We didn't exactly walk down no aisle, or anything like that, but we been together now for going on eight years. The kids needed anything, Laquinta knew she could come to me."

Big Boy lets go with a burp that shakes the windows and probably scares the neighborhood dogs.

"But," he says, holding up a finger that's bigger than my thumbs, "I want to make sure they got the right one, the one that really did kill Artesian. Don't want nobody gettin' away with it while an innocent man takes the fall."

I am touched that Big Boy is so concerned with the welfare of a white man who might or might not have raped and killed his surrogate son.

I ask him if he has any reason to think that Sam McNish isn't guilty.

"I have my reasons to think he didn't do it."

When I press him on what exactly the damn reasons might be, he just looks away and says, "It's a feeling I got, is all. Just a feeling in my gut."

I ask him if he's ever heard about Frosty. He doesn't make the connection for a few seconds, and then he chuckles.

"Everybody knows about Frosty," he says, finishing off his fries and reaching for the soda. "At least everybody where I come from does. Didn't anybody much take it seriously, even in my neighborhood. But people been talking about Frosty for years. The police might have looked into it at one time, but nobody ever found nothing."

So, I ask him, if there really is a Frosty, is it possible that he's still out there, and that he's the one who killed those kids? It's a leap, of course, to assume they were killed, since nobody ever found the bodies of the first four.

"Well," Big Boy says, peeling a stick of Teaberry gum and popping it in his mouth, "the Lord has a way of taking care of things like that. Might not be in the here and now, but eventually."

For a guy who probably has dispatched a party or two himself and has no doubt supervised a shitload of other mortal departures, he seems a bit sanguine.

So, I ask, where would somebody start looking if he wanted to bring a little justice to Artesian Cole and those four other boys, to say nothing of saving Sam McNish's ass?

"Oh," Big Boy says, "I don't know, but the evidence is out there somewhere. It just takes a smart newspaper man like yourself to find it."

He gives one of the young bloods up front a nonverbal message, just the tiniest sideways movement of his head, and my door is opened for me a few seconds later. Interview over.

"Take care now," Big Boy says as I exit his car. "Do good."

It sounds almost like an order.

THE SPIRIT of the season has not descended upon the newsroom.

Today we got our Christmas bonuses. There was a time, now but a dim, bittersweet memory for me and my more aged comrades, when you could pay off your Christmas bills with the company's yuletide largesse. When we tell the young'uns about it, they either don't believe it or just get pissed off.

We always hope for, but never expect, a return to those thrilling days of yesteryear.

This year, the company managed to exceed our worst expectations.

"Twenty-five fucking dollars," Sally Velez says. "A twenty-five-dollar gift certificate from Food Lion. Jesus, I couldn't pull a good drunk on that."

Last year, it was fifty dollars. Doesn't take a math major to figure out what we'll get next year.

I point out that Food Lion's wine is pretty cheap. Sally does not appear to be appeased.

They're making Wheelie and two of his assistant managing editors hand out the envelopes as they thank us for our service. When our editor sees me, he makes his way over, looking as sheepish as a man should look when he's giving Food Lion gift certificates for Christmas bonuses.

"It's all they're giving anybody," he says. I tell him not to worry about it. Nobody expects anything from the company these days anyhow. I'm no MBA, but it seems to me that not giving us anything at all, just pretending Christmas bonuses never existed, would be better for morale than this. But why worry about morale when you wish everybody would just get mad and quit anyhow, thus avoiding the inconvenience of two weeks' severance pay?

Sarah tells me that Enos Jackson took his gift certificate and regifted it to the semihomeless guy who perches outside our building, as soon as the guy assured him he could get to a Food Lion. Maybe I just got an idea for a Christmas present for Awesome Dude.

I talk with Sarah about the Children of God story. She seems a little miffed that I talked to Stella Barnes, wondering somewhat profanely why she even bothered to track the woman down.

"There's always something else you can get in a second interview," I tell her, adding that it was good to get in the front door and interview the woman face-to-face.

"So what did that get you?"

I note that Ms. Barnes seems to be the kind of person who really likes to please.

Sarah gets it after a beat or two.

"Oh. Damn, Willie, you're not going to sleep with her, are you?"

I'm offended, or at least pretend to be.

"I am a professional journalist," I harrumph as she tries to suppress a smirk. "And besides, she's not my type."

"Excuse me. I didn't know you were so persnickety. Oh, yeah, that's right. You're going steady now."

I always thought that, when I reached a certain age, I would be a respected mentor to the newsroom's young turks. Obviously, fifty-four isn't old enough.

I tell Sarah about the command appearance for Big Boy Sunday.

"He's the kid's mother's boyfriend? Jesus, we haven't written that yet, have we?"

No, I tell her, we haven't, because nobody told us before for sure. For now, he'll still be a "family friend."

Even knowing as little as she does about Big Boy, she is as puzzled as I was about why he even cares whether Sam McNish lives or dies.

"We do have a story, though," I tell her, "one that's going to knock people's dicks—excuse me, socks—off."

She nods her head. She knows what I'm talking about.

"Yeah. Frosty. If that doesn't sell some papers, I'll give back my whole Christmas bonus."

CHAPTER NINE

Saturday

Frosty has pretty much lit Richmond up. Everybody loves a mysterious mass murderer as long as he's not in their neighborhood. The comments under the story that bore mine and Sarah's bylines hit triple figures by the time I'd had a cup of coffee and a smoke. Even at Joe's Inn I can't escape it.

The old Oregon Hill gang gets together at Joe's on Saturdays when we can. If any of us is early enough to get the big table in the back, we can sit there for two or three hours, tell lies, drink three-dollar Bloody Marys and even order a little grub. One time, McGonnigal figured that, if you toted up the amount of food we ate and the cheap booze we consumed, it came out to about eight dollars an hour per customer. The wait staff must love us. At least we tip big.

Abe and I get there after everyone else. To my surprise, Cindy's at the big table. I guess Andy invited her. We do allow for special guests on occasion, and Andy Peroni's little sister is pretty special to me.

They let me squeeze in next to my main squeeze, who asks if I'm surprised to see her and manages to brush her hand against Little Willie under the table.

The talk is mostly about Artesian Cole's murder, and more specifically about Sam McNish. Since Cindy is the only one of us in his age bracket, her brother and McGonnigal pepper her with questions. One of the things I like about Cindy is that she plays it pretty close to the vest. No one at the table except me knows her contribution to my story. I don't think anyone, even Andy, remembers that she worked for Grace of God for a while.

Some guy I don't know but who thinks he knows me plops his ass down uninvited across the table. He looks like he might have gone straight from clubbing to an all-night diner to Joe's.

"This Frosty guy," he says, and I can smell his breath across the table, "is he for real, or is that just some shit you all make up to sell papers?"

I inform him that we almost never make up stories.

"Aw, bullshit," he says. Obviously, he already knows what he knows and just needs a little confirmation. "The cops already got the guy that did it, that faggot over at that damn so-called church. You all must be covering for him."

At this point, I'm about to come across the table and try to serve up a helping of whip-ass, which might be the excuse Joe's has been looking for to make better use of the big table we're hogging. Custalow probably saves me from embarrassment, injury, eviction, or all three. He reaches over, puts his big right arm around the guy's neck, and whispers something into his ear.

The guy looks at Abe and sees something that registers. He doesn't say another word, just gets up and leaves. Doesn't even look back.

I give Custalow my best WTF look.

He shrugs his somewhat massive shoulders.

"I just told him this was a private gathering and I'd appreciate it if he'd leave."

It's possible, I guess. Custalow, when he gets that pissed-off Indian look, like he's about to go all Little Bighorn on you, sometimes can convey his message in a very few words.

We give our missing fifth, Goat Johnson, a call on his cell. We put him on speakerphone. Francis Xavier Johnson is no doubt on his knees blowing some prospective donor to that college in Ohio he presides over. The way he speaks, low and circumspect, makes us think he is among a group of scholars who would be appalled at his redneck, white-socks, and blue-collar roots.

I remind him that I have memories of him pissing into the convertible of a boy from the West End who had had the temerity to date an Oregon Hill girl.

He must have stepped into an unoccupied room by now, because he reminds me that I've done everything he's done, in triplicate.

True dat, I concede, but nobody expects any better of journalists.

He laughs and promises to come back to Richmond and kick my ass in the near future.

"We still on for tomorrow?" Cindy asks me as we're finally relinquishing our table.

Absolutely, I tell her. Cindy wants to go to Colonial Williamsburg to "get in the Christmas spirit." It might take more than bread pudding and fools dressed up like Patrick Henry to do that for me, but I'm game. We can blow my Christmas bonus if there are any Food Lions in Williamsburg.

"You can get a lot of baloney and cheese for twenty-five dollars," I tell her.

"I get a lot of baloney all the time, hooked up with you," she replies. "I'm expecting a little better cut of meat tomorrow."

I thank her again for her insight into Sam McNish and Stella Barnes. I give her the short version of my chat with Ms. Barnes.

"I think she liked me," I add.

"She hasn't been around you enough to know any better."

I drop Custalow off back at the Prestwould and go to check on my blood kin. As Abe gets out of the Honda, I ask him what exactly he said to the jerk back at Joe's.

"I'd like to know," I tell him, "so I can use that line next time some guy wants to kick my ass."

"It's not what you say," Custalow explains as he shuts the door. "It's how you say it."

At my mother's house, Peggy, Andi, and young William are (a) mildly stoned, (b) washing clothes, and (c) sleeping. Awesome Dude is out and about. Despite the fact that he has a warm English basement in which to sleep these days, compliments of my mother, he's still a wee bit feral.

"Quip's coming by later," Andi tells me. "He wants to see William."

I ask her if she wants me to be there when that happens. I still wouldn't mind doing some impromptu dental work on the guy who knocked up my little girl.

"Dad," she says, dragging the word out like an exasperated ninth grader, "he is the father. He's not a bad guy. He's just not quite grown up yet."

"He seems like an OK guy," Peggy, ever the astute observer of humanity, offers.

I am slightly concerned that Andi is defending the guy she definitely did not want to marry when the rabbit died, but what the hell. What has taking the high road gotten her?

A berth in a lower-middle-class rental in Oregon Hill that she shares with her grandmother and a guy whose legal name is Awesome Dude. She's tending bar and trying to jump through the last hoops between her and a degree that won't likely get her a better paying job than bartender or waitress. At least as long as I keep my sorry-ass job, she won't come out of VCU with a five-figure debt, which seems to be the standard these days.

I guess some of my irritation with Thomas Jefferson Blandford V is that he and his rich-ass family might take this darling boy sleeping in front of me out of my orbit and into the cloistered West End, where the black side of his family would become an embarrassment to him some day, the source of self-deprecating humor.

Yeah, being around the upper crust does make my butt itch a little. So shoot me.

SPEAKING OF shooting and other forms of mayhem, my wishes for a slow Saturday are dashed before I even get to the paper.

Sally Velez calls me when I'm a block away and says they've had an apparent homicide. In Richmond, this normally would be slightly more startling than telling me the sun came up in the east.

This one, though, is different. The victim is one James N. Alderman. He served a few terms on city council. He was head honcho at the seminary for God knows how many years. He still teaches a class on religion at VCU, and Andi tells me you have to be a senior to even have a chance of getting into it. He's also the only Pulitzer Prize winner I know of, or knew of, in our area. We sure as hell haven't won any at the paper. Alderman got his for a highly acclaimed book no one

I'm aware of has read, on the origins of the Old Testament. Hell, I thought God just dictated it to Abraham. That's what I think they told me in Sunday school.

At any rate, James N. Alderman is not a man to be relegated to an obit on B3. He's A1, all the way.

Sally is still talking to me when I walk in the front door and am waved past by Shorty Cole's replacement, an old white guy who doesn't look like he's toting.

This story seems pretty sure to knock the feature piece on the VCU basketball coach's wife, the paper's first nonalabaster Christmas mother, off the top of the front page. I tell Sally she can hang up and tell me the rest of it in person as soon as I make my way up the elevator and clock in.

When I get to her desk, she says I need to go right back out. Baer is already on his way there, but I might know somebody who'll tell me what really happened.

"We got a tip," Sally tells me. "Whoever put it on our blog said there was blood all over the place. We know he's almost certainly a homicide and the cops are on it like dogs on a hambone, but they aren't telling us shit, as usual."

Why she thinks anyone in a uniform would talk to me is a mystery. I'm pretty sure L.D. Jones has my name at the top of his "do not acknowledge" list. Well, I can always try. And thinking that Mark Baer might be poaching a story that should belong to the cops reporter is enough to inspire me.

Alderman's house is on Seminary Avenue, one of our fair city's prettier streets, up on the North Side. The big oaks and sycamores that line it, planted long ago, make it look like you're somewhere much more exotic and European than Richmond. Even now, with all the leaves off, the branches hover overhead like a protective covering.

Apparently, they didn't do much to protect James N. Alderman.

I'm not usually that thrilled to see Gillespie, a cop with whom I have some bittersweet history. But today I'm happy he's here. He might, if I kiss his butt with enough sincerity, talk to me.

Gillespie seems to have actually gained weight. This shouldn't be surprising, since he seems to spend much of his working shift at the Sugar Shack, where people, including me, stand in the cold for half an hour to buy donuts. The last time I saw him here, his car was parked outside, and I saw him order half a dozen maples and half a dozen samosas. When I came out five minutes later with my dozen glazed, he was still in the parking lot. He looked like he had two samosas in his mouth already.

I tapped on the window. He did not look especially glad to see me.

"Gillespie," I told him, "you are a cliché." I'm not sure he knew what it meant, but I sent him a dozen from Sugar Shack two days later at the station. You never know when you'll need a friend.

I catch him standing in the front yard. There are about three times as many cops here as you'd need for a bomb threat, let alone the death of one old man.

"Did you get the donuts?" I ask him as I come up from behind.

"Yeah," he says. "I shared 'em with the other guys. Didn't tell 'em who they were from."

Knowing Gillespie, he probably had eight and shared the other four, but it's hard to be a Sugar Shack sharer.

I cut to the chase.

"What happened?"

He leads me around the corner, past a huge boxwood that should shield us from anyone who might object to a cop conversing with a nosy-ass reporter.

They found him, Gillespie says, shortly after noon. One of the neighbors had gone over to take him some leftovers—apparently Mr. Alderman wasn't much on cooking for himself. When the neighbor looked in through a window around back, he saw the victim, or what was left of him.

"The guy said he barfed in the yard," Gillespie says. "He was pretty shook up."

Gillespie said they found Alderman's thumbs lying near the chair where he was tied. His penis and balls had been stuffed in his mouth. There were sundry other stab marks all over his body and a couple of gunshot wounds for good measure. From the mess he made of his Turkish carpet, he seemed to have bled to death.

"I'm thinking he probably was glad to die by the time they got through with him."

I'm thinking Gillespie is right. I feel safe in using as much of the grisly details as our editors think our readers can stand. Gillespie can be a fuckup, but he's about as devious as a Labrador retriever. What he told me I'm sure is the truth. The only question, of course, is why.

I approach the chief, who tells me it's—repeat after me—"an ongoing investigation." I pretend to be disappointed. He doesn't even pretend to give a damn about that. I am buoyed by the vision of the chief, tucking into his Sunday morning bacon and eggs, when he reads: "Chief Larry Doby Jones refused to comment on the killing. However, sources within the department said . . ." I owe Gillespie another dozen, at least.

THE NEWSROOM is humming for a Saturday afternoon. I see to my chagrin that Rita Dominick is at large. This one no doubt has the big boys really charged up. Five black kids

disappearing and maybe slaughtered is nothing compared to
the death of James N. Alderman. Our longtime core readership, old white folks, is dropping like flies, with families
buying two-column obits and canceling dad's subscription at
the same time. However, that's still who we're playing to.

"Drop that Frosty stuff and get on this one," Dominick
says as she comes striding up to me like George Patton on
amphetamines. I think it just makes her all tingly to speak the
obvious in a loud and grating voice.

When I tell Sally and Sarah what Gillespie told me, not for
attribution, Sally says we probably should run it past Wheelie.

"You know, taste and all that shit."

By the time it's over, our publisher and Wheelie have con-
ferred, with Ms. Dominick doing most of the talking and
Wheelie doing most of the nodding, and it's decided that we
will tiptoe past what she calls "the gruesome details."

OK, fine, I tell Wheelie when he passes that message along
to me, but how come we weren't squeamish about saying the
Cole boy probably was sexually molested?

"Just do it," Wheelie says. "Act like you don't have any
choice, because you don't."

Wheelie reminds me of how hard it is for fifty-four-year-
old heavy smokers to land on their feet.

So we wind up telling our readers that James Alderman
died from stab and gunshot wounds in what appeared to be
a break-in at his North Side home. Enough to jerk the chief's
chain, but not enough to avoid being chickenshit.

The really crazy part is that nothing like this can stay
secret long in a city this size. The neighbor tells ten other
neighbors, who tell ten of their friends each, and so on.
By the time our watered-down version of James Alderman's
demise lands on their doorsteps tomorrow morning, even our
gray West End constituency will be saying, "Duh. I read what

really happened online. Are those guys at the paper asleep?" And that's discounting the very real chance that all the TV stations will have it on the eleven o'clock news. The TV guys don't worry too much about sensitivity.

A couple of shootings with no dirt naps involved comprise the rest of my night. I have time for a few hands of solitaire on the computer. A couple of the guys on the copy desk and I are even able to slip over to Penny Lane. I'm no foodie, but my advice on British grub is: Focus on the beer.

We do that. Two Harps later, I'm back across the street, waiting for something to happen and hoping nothing does.

I'm going through my notes on what are now known as the McNish murders and thinking more about Frosty than about James Alderman, I guess because everyone else seems more focused on the latter, per marching orders from our publisher.

About ten, I decide to give Cindy a call.

She answers on the third ring.

"I'm surprised you're not out on the town," I tell her.

"How do you know I'm not? Just a sec. Stop that, Lance! Get your hand out of there. People are watching."

"Lance? Really? You know, I can hear your TV in the background. *Masterpiece Theater*, am I right?"

"Busted. I'm saving all my energy for tomorrow. A girl can't go out on the town every night."

It is a problem, my work schedule. When you get off work at one A.M. five nights a week, about the only options are to go home, go to a bar and speed-drink, or go crawl in bed with Cindy. The third option is one I'm becoming very fond of, and I do have a key now, but nobody wants to be awakened on a regular basis in the middle of the night by a reporter's cold feet. Cindy has a part-time job and classes at

VCU, so I try to time my post-midnight visits to coincide with days where she doesn't have to set the alarm clock.

And I know Cindy doesn't sit home waiting for me all those nights. She might even find a pleasing young man, one with a dependable career and sane work hours, on one of those nights. Who could blame her?

We talk a bit about her day and mine. I fill her in on what I know but can't print about the Alderman murder. She seems to agree with our publisher that dismembered body parts are not what she wants with her sausage and eggs.

"That's really amazing, though. I mean the coincidence."

"Coincidence?"

"Yeah. About James Alderman. Happening just, what, eight days after that boy's body was found."

"You're speaking in riddles."

"Oh," she says after a pause, "I thought you knew. About Alderman and the Children of God program. He was a mentor there when I was there, and I'm pretty sure he's still connected. I can't believe you didn't know that. What kind of reporter are you, anyhow?"

Indeed.

CHAPTER TEN

Sunday

To the surprise of no one with any sense, the TV stations did suss out the particulars of James Alderman's death, although not in time for the late-night news. But it was all over their websites by the time I woke up and checked. To make matters more galling, if that's possible, our Internet geeks rewrote the TV stations' versions, which were somewhat misinformed, and put that crap on our site, under my damn byline.

Gillespie isn't the only one out there who either saw or heard about the body, and everybody loves to have access to and dish out information nobody else has. Hell, that's why I'm a newspaperman.

So I have to call our web guru, who's all of twenty-five, blister his ears for a bit, and then send him the details I tried to put in the Sunday paper. He seems neither chastened nor grateful.

It not only looks like we've been beaten by every TV station in town; now a sane person would assume that the paper also got scooped by our online "product," whose producers are in reality good for nothing more than rewriting (and usually butchering) what the actual reporters gather out here in the real world.

I give Kate a call. I can hear Grace singing in the background. It stuns me to realize my ex-wife's daughter is now talking. I wish time would slow the hell down.

I give her the news that James Alderman had links to Sam McNish and the Children of God program.

Her response is somewhat emphatic.

"Is that the same mouth you kiss Grace goodnight with?" I ask.

She tells me to fuck off.

"The guy that was murdered? He worked with McNish? Why the hell didn't he tell us?"

I remind her that James Alderman was somewhat of a nonplayer in current events, just a city icon, until the unfortunate events of yesterday.

"Well," she says, "I definitely have some questions for Mr. McNish."

I gather from her tone that those questions might not wait until the start of the business week.

I tell her I'll check back tomorrow when Cindy and I return from Williamsburg.

"Williamsburg, huh? Must be serious, if she's gotten you to do that Colonial crap. Hell, you never took me there."

I remind her that she, like me at that time, would have preferred to eat a broken Budweiser bottle. She concedes that I'm right, and that she and Mr. Ellis probably will go themselves one day next week, to please Gracie.

"We've changed," I observe.

"Yes. Maybe for the better?"

I'M SUPPOSED to pick Cindy up at ten forty-five. Then, before we leave for Williamsburg, I am doing something I would only do for someone for whom I care a great deal.

I am going to church.

Cindy's not a regular, she assures me, but it's eleven days until Christmas, and she thinks she ought to go. When I suggest that Santa Claus probably will fill her stocking whether she sings hymns on Sunday or not, she just says that it would mean a lot to her if I came with her. She said it in a way that made me think it would also mean a lot if I didn't.

For some reason, Christians seem to associate Christmas with Christ. I can see very little evidence that the holiday and its namesake have much in common anymore. I can't find much sign of a link at the mall, on TV, or anywhere else. I don't expect it to be any different in Colonial Williamsburg. The money changers definitely seem to have the upper hand these days.

But what are you going to do? You're going to put on your least-rumpled sport jacket, a little-used pair of dress pants, and some rarely shined shoes, and do what you have to do.

The church is out in the West End, not far off of West Grace, and I can't help but compare this fine Baptist structure with Grace of God. The parishioners are almost all white and almost all dressed better than I am, which is saying almost nothing at all. God or someone seems to have blessed the church itself.

There's a sanctuary that must seat at least six hundred, from my rough estimate. There are plush little pillows so our butts don't suffer during the sermon. I think McNish's place was using folding chairs. The choir looks radiant in its purple finery. The minister appears to be well-fed and pleased with himself, his congregation, and the whole damn world.

The church has a school connected to it, K through twelve. When Cindy points this out, I refer to it as a segregation academy, which is what a lot of these nonpublic schools started out as. Cindy replies, with a little flint in her tone, I might add, that there are lots of minority students there. Looking around the congregation, I think those minorities might be mostly the kind with two tiger parents prodding them to study harder and seize that full scholarship to MIT, or those whose parents do a lot of the work we "real" Americans would rather not soil our hands with. I don't see evidence, in other words, of many people of my late father's ethnic persuasion.

But the sermon is tolerable and short, and I see that the church is looking for volunteers to go into the backwoods of Southwest Virginia to assist dentists and doctors who occasionally do a pilgrimage down there to help those whose retirement strategy is the lottery and who are on the DGS health plan—Don't Get Sick.

As one who doesn't do much for his fellow man beyond buying him a beer or slipping him a buck when he's standing there staring at me in the intersection while I wait for the light to change, I do not have the high ground.

"So," Cindy says as we're walking back to my car, "that didn't kill you, did it?"

"Not yet. Weren't you afraid lightning would strike you, sitting next to me in church?"

"I like to live dangerously."

On the way to Williamsburg, we make a quick detour to see Philomena and Richard Slade. Richard has put one of those damn blowup Christmas figures in his front yard, a Santa Claus whose maniacal grin is enough to scare the neighborhood kids. Next to it is another one, a nativity scene perhaps done at Philomena's insistence. Richard has strung lights

along the gutters on the front and sides of Momma Phil's
house, and in the living room there's a Christmas tree so big
that it's scraping the ceiling. It's like Richard is trying to make
up for those twenty-eight years he spent wrongfully incarcer-
ated. They probably didn't have a lot of yuletide festivities in
the big house.

We can't stay but a minute; Williamsburg awaits. I have
presents for Philomena and Richard, my links to my father's
darker side of the family. And it would have been suicide to
come here without something for the boys, who have to be
threatened with corporal punishment ("Don't make me get
a switch after you!") to keep them from opening their gifts
right damn now. And, of course, I got Chanelle a little something as well. Philomena has something for me too. She says
this might be her son's last Christmas living in her home. He
seems to have found someone to share the rest of his so-far
star-crossed life with, which comes about as close to quash-
ing my inner Grinch as anything I've experienced so far this
season.

Richard walks us back to the car. He seems to have something on his mind.

"I hear you've been talking to Big Boy," he says.

I ask him how in the world he knows that.

He shrugs.

"Word gets around. It isn't that big a town. Him and me,
we know some of the same people."

Richard says that Big Boy Sunday's exploits made their
way inside the gates at Greensville, where some of his soldiers
wound up.

"He grew up right near here. He was just making his
bones when I got sent away, but there was always stories.
Inmates would talk about things Big Boy had done.

"They'd always laugh and say Big Boy was too smart to ever get caught for anything serious, never would do much time. They wouldn't have talked about it, but we were all home boys, you know."

I wonder what Richard's driving at. He comes to the point.

"Thing is, he really is a bad dude. I know he's got a special interest in that boy that got killed, and I know what he is capable of doing. I'm just saying, don't get in a situation where you're on his bad side. He has messed some people up."

When I tell him that Big Boy seems to want me to find the real killer, and that he gives every impression of not believing that Sam McNish is it, Richard seems surprised.

"Well," he says at last, "he's got his reasons. Big Boy's always got his reasons, and, believe me, what he wants and what you want might not be the same thing."

I tell him he doesn't have to sell me on the lethal potential of Big Boy Sunday. A guy who can scare people enough to kill for him and then go to prison without fingering him has my attention. I promise Richard that I will proceed with caution.

He claps me on the shoulder and says, "You do that, Willie. We don't want anything to happen to you. You're family."

I thank him for that, and I really mean it. My involvement in a story two years ago would wind up making me a party to Richard Slade's exoneration for the murder of the woman whose long-ago testimony short-circuited his life. It has brought me an unexpected gift: the gift of family.

I will never know the late Artie Lee, the father I never had. Maybe I like him better for not knowing him. Now, though, I at least have the vestiges of him in Philomena's stories. And then there are the twins.

"Those boys," Philomena said today after invoking the switch threat again. "They're just like Artie Lee was when he was that age."

We check in at the Williamsburg Lodge. The price is only tolerable if you consider the alternative.

"Look at it this way," Cindy says, "we're saving three hundred dollars a night by not staying at the inn."

Great, I say. If we stay for a week, we'll be more than two thousand bucks to the good.

We do all the touristy crap. We walk around the re-created Colonial town that half these dummies from Ohio or Arkansas think is the real thing.

A lot of them seem to have skipped history class too.

"Those Pilgrims," I hear one fat guy from Up North tell his wife, "they really knew how to build shit."

I'm freezing my butt off, the smoke from those outdoor fires is making me sneeze, and the shops are full of overpriced stuff that nobody needs. When I look over and see Cindy, though, she looks like a kid on Christmas morning. Time to quit whining and suck it up. We'll call it Cindy Day.

Before dinner, I check in with Kate again.

She and Marcus have, as I figured, already been to the jail to have a Sunday chat with Sam McNish.

"He was surprised that we would care to know that Alderman worked there some," Kate says. "He said Alderman was just doing what a lot of other people did: helping out with the mentoring. He'd known him since he was a student at Union Seminary. Said Alderman was like his mentor."

McNish was, Kate says, extremely upset over Alderman's death.

"He said something about bad things happening to good people, said he would pray for whoever was depraved enough to kill a good man like James Alderman."

"But he didn't think there could have been any connection between the Cole kid's murder and Alderman's?"

"He said he couldn't imagine what it could be. Maybe he's right."

And maybe he's not. We have a lot of murders in Richmond, but most of them are of the tragic but mundane variety. Husband kills wife. Drug buyer kills drug seller or vice versa. There's usually a reason. Maybe you got your ass into a dangerous situation. Maybe you married the wrong guy. But when we have two killings of the seemingly blameless in this spectacular a fashion in this short a period of time, the smart money is not on coincidence.

"He wants to talk to you," Kate says. She doesn't seem very happy to be telling me that.

"When?"

"Whenever you can. Tomorrow, if you're back from Ye Olde Williamsburg by then."

"Why?"

"He seems to trust you, Willie. I don't know, maybe it's an Oregon Hill thing. Maybe he just doesn't know you all that well."

Sources, I want to tell my ex-wife and present landlady, could always trust me.

Wives? Now that was a different story.

WE HAVE dinner at the inn. Cindy goes for the lobster bisque and chateaubriand. I get the oysters Rockefeller and the crab cakes. You really can't go wrong with crab cakes, as long as you don't drift any farther south than the North Carolina state line. I think I had a pecan torte for dessert. I am not sure.

The trouble started right after we got back from our stroll and I checked in again with Kate.

I blame it on timing. We had a couple of hours to kill between a little horizontal in-room entertainment and our dinner reservation. I was feeling good. I was at the end of a truly virtuous day—church with my sweetie, bringing gifts to my cousins, springing for an expensive night at a joint where I really didn't want to be in the first place.

When I start feeling good, sometimes things start to go really bad.

WE GO to the lounge where we're staying. It's happy hour. Maybe I notice Cindy frowning a little as I have my second bourbon on the rocks. Usually, I drink the kind of stuff that can be watered down at no great loss in quality. If it tastes like crap, water can make it taste only half as much like crap. But this is a special occasion, a Knob Creek kind of occasion, and anybody who'd adulterate Knob Creek with water would put an ice cube in a good Bordeaux. The bartender is generous, and I start feeling even better. I get into a conversation with some guy who wants to talk about the Civil War. The Civil fucking War is usually a topic I find about as appealing as genital herpes. If you live in my neck of the woods, you get beaten to death with Waw of Nawthen Aggression, especially by the apologists who claim it was about states' rights instead of keeping my direct ancestors in chains.

Now, though, chatting with this schmuck from Pennsylvania I just met, I find myself trying to defend the indefensible. I guess he just rubbed me the wrong way. He says something, as I recall, about the best thing that ever happened to the

South was losing the Civil War, and I say something about how I'd rather be in jail in Richmond than mayor of whatever shithole, rusted-out, Polack icebox of a town he was from. It's starting to get a bit tense, and I'm trying to order my third Knob Creek, when his wife pulls him away and Cindy does the same to me.

"Don't do this," I remember her saying to me.

But when you're hot, you're hot. By then, it's time to go to dinner. Over somewhat strong protest, I have another KC before we order. But I'm still in what I feel is the Good Willie zone, the one where you're the life of the party but not yet wearing the lampshade. Sure, I'd been a little loud, a little truculent back there at the bar, but I'm getting my second wind now. I assure Cindy that everything is going to be OK.

As is often the case, I am wrong.

Cindy, who had one Scotch and soda back at happy hour, orders another just to stay in the same orbit as me, because the only thing worse than being with a drunk is being sober while you're with a drunk.

Then, we order a nice malbec with dinner and finish that. Well, mostly, I finish it. And then I order another one. I guess I don't notice that I'm drinking almost all of that one, or that Cindy isn't talking very much if at all.

When I order a Cognac with my dessert instead of following Cindy's example and switching to coffee, she puts her napkin down on the table and stands up.

"I'll be back in the room," she says.

I put my hand on her arm, hoping to persuade her to stay. She tells me to let go. I don't, still thinking I can charm her. I'm feeling pretty damn charming by now.

And then this guy at the next table asks her if she needs any help. I tell him that if we need his fucking help, we'll ask for it. He says something equally rude back at me, and I take a swing at him. From the shiner that greets me in the mirror when I come to the next morning, he must have given me more or less what I deserved.

They get me out of the Regency Room and on my way as quickly as possible. Just when I think things can't get any worse, I hear some guy a few tables over say, "Isn't that Willie Black, that reporter from Richmond?"

You help an old lady across the street and nobody notices, but just try duking it out with some tourist in a good restaurant fifty miles from home and you're a celebrity.

I don't remember how I got back to the room, although the dirt on my pants, mixed with the vomit, tells me it was not a smooth voyage.

CHAPTER ELEVEN

Monday

The sun wakes me up. The clock reads nine fifteen. Cindy is gone.

Who the hell could blame her?

As it turns out, she called her brother, my old pal Andy Peroni, sometime after I passed out last night. He came and got her. I found all this out from Andy when he called my cell phone about ten this morning. He assured me that he and Cindy made sure I was breathing before they left. I guess I should be grateful for that. Cindy doesn't want me dead. She just wants me out of her damn life.

I have screwed up before. I'm a heavy favorite to screw up again. This time, though, the price is steep. After an unfortunate incident at O'Toole's last year, I was afraid I had lost the best thing that had happened to me in a long time. I worked hard to get Cindy Peroni back. And now I've blown it again.

"I don't know, man," Andy says when I get up the nerve to ask him the lay of the land regarding his sister. "Damn, Willie. You could fuck up Christmas."

It was always just a saying, an expression that meant you were capable of ruining just about anything. With Our Lord's birthday now ten days away, it sounds pretty literal.

"Maybe," he adds, "you ought to get some help. I can put you in touch with some people."

I tell him I'll sleep on it, but after I hang up, I just toss and turn, then finally get up and face the cold, cruel day. It is hard to imagine calling Cindy. It is harder to imagine her not hanging up. She told me last year that she wasn't going to let me put frown wrinkles on her pretty face, that she'd leave me first. Forewarned is fucked.

When I check out, the guy at the front desk seems to avoid eye contact, as if all Williamsburg knows about my one-round bout in the Regency Room.

Work might not make you free, but it will let you put a temporary mental slipcover over some of your more shameful moments. So I call Kate to see when I might have a few words with a man who has bigger problems than I do.

"I think you can see him pretty much anytime. When are you coming back? Did you have a good time in Williamsburg?"

"Not exactly."

"Oh. Sorry."

Kate kind of knows the kind of "not exactly" good time Willie Black can have. She's been along for a few of them.

McNish is ushered in half an hour after I get back, about one thirty. I have sunk so low that a man arrested for allegedly raping and murdering a schoolboy has to ask me if I'm OK.

He seems to be in fine spirits, all things considered. The only thing that concerns him is James Alderman.

"Who in the world would kill him? All he ever did was work to make the world better."

I note that the world is full of injustice. Sometimes people even get arrested for crimes they didn't commit.

He waves his hands as if batting away the notion that his petty troubles could hold a light to the murder of James Alderman.

"This will all straighten itself out," he says. "The truth will out."

Sometimes, I suggest, the truth needs a little help.

"Tell me about James Alderman."

When he hesitates, I explain that I am supposed to write something about the deceased for Tuesday's paper, which is true. However, I also am trying to figure out how his death might connect with the Cole boy's murder. As I said, I believe that coincidences are the exception.

McNish goes on for twenty minutes about how Alderman helped him find his way when he was a young Ivy League grad at that fork between the high road and the one that makes you rich.

"He took me around to some of the poorer neighborhoods and showed me how unjust the world was. I thought we had it rough growing up in Oregon Hill, Willie, but some of these kids, they were starting at such a disadvantage that it was hard to see how they could ever catch up.

"And it's still like that, for some of them."

Alderman was his mentor while McNish was in divinity school. He says that he always knew, through the years, that he could go to James Alderman whenever he was having a crisis of faith, or even something as mundane as a crisis of cash.

"He paid our heating bills two different times when we were short. And he insisted that we not pay him back.

"My dad wasn't around, so I guess you could say James Alderman was a father figure. But not just for me. He was there for a lot of others too."

I ask him if Alderman had ever had any contact with Artesian Cole.

He seems surprised by the question.

"No, I don't think so," he says. "At least, not any more than with any of the other boys."

He explains that Alderman did come to Grace of God once a week to talk with the boys about spiritual matters.

"These kids, they have bigger problems than learning the Old and New Testaments, but we do try to bring a little religion into their studies once in a while."

He manages to dredge up a smile.

"After all, we are a church."

I ask if Alderman was there the day the boy disappeared. He thinks for a moment and then says he's sure he wasn't.

"You think there's some connection between these two murders."

It's a statement, not a question.

I tell him I don't know, which is the truth.

"I can't see it," he says. "If there's anybody in the world that was more blameless than Artesian Cole, it was James Alderman. There can't be a person in this world so depraved he would do something like that to those two people."

I know McNish has seen a lot, but a few weeks on the night cops beat might temper his belief in the goodness of human nature.

It occurs to me, as we talk, that I'm as sure of Sam McNish's innocence as I am that the sun rises in the east. He's shown no interest in his own well-being, no anger at being thrown in jail and accused of about the worst damn thing you could accuse a person of. His belief that "truth will out" strikes me as both charming and almost fatally naive.

He seems more concerned with my dissolute state than with his own future.

"You ought to take better care of yourself," he says as I'm leaving.

"Yeah, I get that a lot."

I'M GLAD Custalow isn't in when I get back to the Prestwould. My other buds from Oregon Hill gossip like schoolgirls. I'm sure that my sublessee already has been informed about my misadventure in Williamsburg. He won't lecture me. Hell, Abe was living in the park when I found him. But he does have a way of making you feel you have fallen short. He doesn't have to say a word, just gives you that once-over look and a shake of the head, and I'm not quite up to that right now.

I am allegedly off today, but it's probably better if I keep busy.

So I take a quick shower, doing my best to avoid any mirrors, and head back out.

Leaving the Prestwould involves going through our ornate, Oriental-carpeted lobby, which can be a quiet, peaceful interlude before hitting the mean streets. Or it can be like it is today.

Since I slinked up to my unit two hours ago, bedlam has descended on the lobby. I had forgotten that this is the day we've all been invited by the social committee to put up the Christmas tree, which is a monster. I don't know how they got it in the front door. A dozen residents are, with varying degrees of competency, decorating the tree. The Prestwould is one of the few places in Richmond where being fifty-four years old makes you a youngster. And, since the tree is being put up in the middle of the afternoon, when most of the unretired Prestwouldians are at work, the average age of the party now attacking our yule tree is trending octogenarian.

Feldman, Mr. McGrumpy, is on a ladder, apparently angling for a lawsuit. Two women in their early eighties are trying to hold the ladder steady while Feldman, who must be about five foot four by now, reaches as far as his superannuated arms can stretch. He has a star in his hand.

Watching him teeter up there is more than I can stand. Finally, I coax him down and put the damn star on myself, to great applause from the ladies and a scowl from McGrumpy, who protests that he could have done it.

"You look like hell," he says. I tell him I'll be better tomorrow, the implication being that he won't.

I turn and am about to head out the door when I almost run into Clara Westbrook.

The Prestwould's grande dame is offering me a cup of eggnog, which she assures me is spiked to full adult strength. Normally, that would be enough to keep me around for a few minutes. Today, I beg off, telling Clara that I've already consumed my weekly limit of booze.

Clara is one of our building's prize possessions. She organizes the parties, gives sage advice only when asked, and has never, in my memory, told the same story twice. If I ever get to my ninth decade, I want to be Clara Westbrook.

Among her many positive attributes: She knows pretty much everyone in town.

"I can't get over Jimmy Alderman," she says, shaking her head.

It takes me a moment to make the connection.

"James Alderman?"

"Yes. I guess he's been James for quite a while," she says. "But he'll always be Jimmy to me."

Part of being a good reporter is knowing when to rearrange your plans. I had my mind set on confronting L.D. Jones and forcing him to listen to my heartfelt belief that he has an innocent man in his lockup. Sometimes, though, it's better to turn off the engine, shut the fuck up, and listen.

I lead Clara over to a couple of chairs halfway down the lobby from where McGrumpy is again trying to kill himself with the aid of a ladder.

"You've known James Alderman a long time?"

She laughs.

"I've known a lot of people a long time, Willie. I've had a long time to know people."

She tells me about how they ran in the same circles, although she was several years older. She said she runs into him from time to time, or did at least. They belonged to some of the same clubs.

I ask her if Alderman had ever had any kind of problems.

"Like what?"

"I don't know. Did he drink? Did he have anybody he owed money to? Any enemies?"

Clara frowns.

"It isn't good to speak ill of the dead, Willie."

I tell her about my concerns over Artesian Cole and James Alderman, both with connections to Grace of God and the Children of God program, being dispatched in such awful fashion within a few days of each other.

Clara is quiet for a few seconds.

"I probably shouldn't repeat this," she says, breaking the silence.

If people didn't repeat what they shouldn't, where would your good, faithful journalist be?

She starts telling me about something that happened twenty years ago. As always with Clara, this is a story I have not heard before.

"There was a boy who lived near Jimmy's house, and he caused quite a stink when he claimed Jimmy tried to grab him and 'do something' to him."

The kid, as Clara remembers it, was a young black boy, "maybe eleven or twelve years old." He said he had been approached by James Alderman walking down the street near Alderman's house. He said Alderman, whom he later identified through a picture, tried to pull him into his van, but that he fought him and ran away.

"Did the paper write anything about it?"

Clara looks at me like I just fell off the turnip truck.

"You didn't just go writing something like that about James Alderman without checking it out," she says. "The boy later retracted his claim. Jimmy Alderman said it was a misunderstanding, that the boy looked like he'd been beaten up in a fight, and he was trying to get him to the hospital."

"Did the police check any of this out? Did the boy look like he'd been in a fight?"

"I don't know, Willie. All I know is that everyone who heard about it knew the boy had to be lying."

She tells me I'd have to be crazy to think that Alderman somehow had anything to do with those murdered kids.

I tell her she's probably right. I'd love to talk to that kid though.

I GET a call from Shorty Cole. He can't tell me how much this job as a bouncer means to him, although he's sure as hell trying. As I walk down the street to my car, I tell him it's nothing. Always glad to do my civic duty, as long as nothing more strenuous than a phone call is involved.

I ask him if he's happy that the police have Artesian's killer behind bars.

He hesitates a moment. Then he says, "I just hope they got the right one."

Mostly, families of the victims of heinous crimes are more of the "kill 'em all and let God sort it out" persuasion. And yet, I have first Big Boy Sunday and now Shorty Cole expressing their concerns that the cops have locked up the wrong guy.

It is definitely time to get inside L.D. Jones's ear, which won't be easy. The chief would much rather talk than listen. And if forced to listen, he'd rather listen to almost anyone other than me.

It is no surprise, then, that I am stonewalled by L.D.'s secretary after she tells him who's waiting to see him. I tell her I can wait. After half an hour, I tell her that the chief has two choices. He can either talk with me right now, or he can read something he probably doesn't want to read in tomorrow's paper.

He makes me cool my heels another fifteen minutes before I am ushered into the *sanctum sanctorum*.

The chief's office has had an extreme makeover since my last visit. Carpet so new I can smell it. A fresh paint job. A fancy-ass chair that looks like it is capable of giving back massages and making coffee. There's a seafaring print on the wall from an artist who is famous enough locally that even I recognize his work. It's an odd choice. I'm pretty sure L.D. can't swim and hates boats.

I comment that it looks like the police business is doing better than the newspaper business these days.

"This place hadn't been renovated in ten years," he says. "It was overdue."

Not to be outdone, I tell him the newsroom staffers got new mousepads last week. I ask him if he still has his bodyguard.

L.D. is not in the mood for small talk, it seems.

"What the hell do you want?"

"You're not going to like it," I tell him.

"If it's coming from you, that's no big surprise."

And so I lay it out, as succinctly as I can:

- Stella Barnes, the woman who raised the alarm about Sam McNish, seems to be a scorned lover who had every reason to hold a grudge, even if she's going all passive-aggressive about it right now.

- James Alderman, our other recent high-profile homicide, once was accused of trying to abduct a boy who was about Artesian Cole's age, although charges were never filed.

- Alderman has worked as a mentor at Children of God.

- There is not one scintilla of hard evidence linking McNish to the crime.

- And, I just don't think there is any way in hell that McNish is capable of doing what he is accused of doing. The basis for that one is gut instinct.

The chief is quiet for a moment. When the folks in Pompeii were suddenly wishing they had volcano insurance, it probably was a little like this.

"Jesus H. Fucking Christ!" he says when the eruption finally comes. "You're crazier than I thought, and that's going some. Let me get this straight. The woman who gave us what seems to be reliable information about McNish might have a motive for talking to us. The late Mr. Alderman once, long ago, was accused of attempted abduction, but the charges were never filed. We don't have a smoking gun yet. And, cherry on top, you've got a feeling."

He pauses to take a breath. I jump in and remind him that I'm not doing that bad on my hunches. I can name a few people who aren't locked up right now because of my hunches.

He looks like he wants to hit me. The shitty mood I'm in today, I almost wish he'd come across that fancy-ass desk and give it a shot.

He takes a deep breath.

"You're not going to print that crap, are you? I mean, even by your standards, you've got nothing to go on. All you're going to do is embarrass a woman who did her civic duty and a dead guy everybody in the whole friggin' town loved. I'm surprised they don't have his damn statue up on Monument Avenue. And you'll make yourself look like more of an asshole than usual."

I have to admit that, no, I'm not going with it right now. That was just a bluff to get into the holy of holies and state my case. We might run something that casts a little doubt on McNish's guilt, but I'm sure the suits would quash anything I wrote about an alleged attempted abduction two decades ago in which no charges were ever brought. Running something like that the day before Alderman's funeral would make even me a little queasy.

He also mentions that all my contentions don't explain how the hell James Alderman turned up extremely dead a few days later. That's the one that will have the mayor and city council really lighting a fire under his ass until somebody gets arrested.

"The thing is, Willie," L.D. says, quieter now, "you don't have a case. We have cases. You have stories. There's a difference. Let us handle the cases and you write the stories."

I have one more request from the chief.

"Would it be possible to find out anything about that boy who accused Alderman of trying to kidnap him? I'd like to talk to him if he's still around."

"You're not going to give up, are you?"

The chief sighs and says he doubts that it is possible to find what I'm looking for. The way he says it, I'm thinking that even if it were possible, it wouldn't be possible.

But he says he'll look into it.

I ask him if his new chair gives blow jobs.

He doesn't say good-bye when I leave.

I check my watch. It's a quarter past four. If I weren't a total fuckup, I'd probably be getting back home with Cindy Peroni about now after a nice breakfast and maybe a tour of Jamestown. We'd be easing into a nice, lazy afternoon of thank-you sex.

In the passenger's seat of my Honda, I see something sparkle. It's one of Cindy's earrings.

I wonder if I'll ever be able to give it back to her in person.

CHAPTER TWELVE

Tuesday

Custalow was through with his custodial duties by the time I got back to the condo yesterday. I was determined to give Penny Lane or anywhere else with a license to serve alcohol a wide berth. He didn't say anything about my Williamsburg mishap, but I could tell he'd heard.

"Go ahead," I said during a commercial while we watched a *Law and Order* episode that was rerunning for the umpteenth time. "Say it."

"What?"

"What you're thinking, dammit."

He set down his beer. Abe is a bear; the Miller looks like a pony bottle in his big, work-scarred hands.

"Willie, you got me off the street. I'll never say anything bad about you, man."

"I can take it."

So he said it.

"You aren't going to have it any better than Cindy Peroni. Even when you're sober, she's out of your league. If there ever was an incentive to not screw up, she'd be it."

I agreed with him. And I appreciated the fact that he didn't suggest that I need help. Some things are obvious.

Custalow's a keeper. More than one Prestwouldian has thanked me for bringing him in from the cold. He earns his keep by being the best custodian our tired-ass building has ever had. And he helps me stay under shelter myself. Kate's not letting me live here for free, and she's raised the rent on me once already.

"By the way," he said when I got up to fetch myself a cold hot dog, "if you're done with her, do you mind if I give her a call?"

Custalow pretty much never smiles. You have to know when he's kidding.

TODAY, SARAH has the latest on McNish and Grace of God. It isn't good. The big house on West Grace has been vandalized. Somebody spray-painted it and tried to start a fire inside that fortunately went out on its own before it could spread.

Children of God is, for all intents and purposes, dead, along with the church McNish built from nothing. Sarah talked with a couple of mothers who brought their sons by after school, hoping that somehow the mentoring program was still breathing. There was a sign on the door saying that classes were suspended "for the foreseeable future." And then, sometime after dark, the vandals struck. A kindly neighbor said the church had always been a bad idea, that the neighborhood had tried to get it shut down for years.

"It's not like those kids don't have schools already that we're paying taxes for," is the way he put it.

I've been to some of the schools on the poor side of town. If the guy who was quoted ever visited one of those under-staffed facilities full of asbestos, mold, and kids who were raised by wolves, he'd be thanking God for the kind of deal McNish was running.

Sarah tracked down one of the assistants at the school. The aide wouldn't talk on the record. Not for attribution, she said that pretty much all the funding for the church and school had dried up, and that people who worked there were getting death threats.

She also said, under cover of anonymity, that she would bet her life savings that Sam McNish was innocent. Hell, maybe if I were getting death threats, I'd go underground too.

I call Sarah and tell her what I've learned about the late Mr. Alderman and the mystery child from more than two decades ago.

"Holy crap. Do you think the cops would have any records?"

"None that they're going to bust a gut to find for me. But I might be able to back-door it."

"Your 'unnamed source'?"

I nod my head. It unnerves me a little that Sally Velez, my editor, knows about Peachy Love. I sure as hell don't want anyone else knowing, or even thinking hard about it.

I have to do a piece leading up to the Alderman funeral tomorrow, which promises to be standing room only. After I get through praising him, though, and before I put on my night cops hat, I will be looking for some material that might not go in the authorized biography.

As LUCK would have it, Peachy Love is taking the week off to get ready for Christmas. I call her home number. She asks me where the hell I've been, and I tell her the usual lie about being busy as hell, was planning to call her, blah, blah, blah. I know that if I go over to her place right now, I'll wind up letting Little Willie take charge. He's already whispering to me, "Cindy's left you, man. Let's go for the gusto."

But something, either hope or conscience, makes me tell Peachy I'm stuck at work and can't come over right now.

I do, though, need a favor.

I explain about the story Clara Westbrook told me, and about the kind of help I need.

Peachy's a little uneasy with the whole thing.

"Damn, Willie. You don't want to go digging up crap that probably doesn't matter. It probably was a bunch of bullshit back then. The boy took back his story, right?"

"That's what they tell me. But I wonder if he did it out of the goodness of his heart."

"Well, I doubt there'd be anything on file about that. Some of the files got lost last time we moved. And with somebody as big as that Alderman guy, I wouldn't be surprised if those files didn't burn themselves up anyhow."

She pauses.

"But I could check around. If I can find a cop that was working back then, maybe somebody would know something."

Thank God for Peachy Love. We are losing so many of our best and brightest reporters these days because they look around one day and say, "Holy shit! I'm thirty-two years old and I can't afford to rent a place that doesn't come with cockroaches."

And so they take jobs as flacks. They go to work for universities or charitable societies or businesses, all of which, at one time or another, need somebody who's good at spinning lies so they look like facts. Who better to hide the truth than someone who was trained to dig it out?

I don't blame them for leaving. If you go to work for one of the really bad ones, maybe a tobacco company or a big utility, you can literally double your salary. You just have to take all the mirrors out of your house. Hell, I might have left already, but who wants a middle-aged "media specialist" who drinks and smokes and isn't either circumspect or pretty. Newspapers have made "journalist" such an unrewarding occupation that their staffs consist mostly of old farts like me, stuck here like polar bears on a melting ice floe, and the kids. I wonder how much longer Sarah Goodnight will stick around.

But Peachy jumped ship before newspapers stopped giving raises. She simply thought it would be fun to work with cops all day, for some damn reason. And when she left the newsroom, she didn't leave her ethics behind. Oh, she does a good job of keeping the public informed, and she does a serviceable job of not keeping the public informed when L.D. Jones doesn't think the taxpayers need to know. But Peachy is smart, and honest. She knows when something needs to be leaked, for the good of the city if not the chief's peace of mind. That's where I come in. I hope L.D. never figures out who the mole is. I, Peachy, and the city of Richmond will be poorer for it if that happens.

I know she'll let me know who might help me find that long-ago kid and who'll tell me something he doesn't want the chief to know he told me.

I call my favorite florist and have him send a dozen long-stemmed red roses to Peachy Love from "her secret admirer."

I think about calling Cindy, but I lose my nerve.

IT's a typical Tuesday night. A guy wearing a Salvation Army uniform got his ass kicked about eight when he set up shop in front of a store on Broad Street. Some of the locals got suspicious, because they'd never seen a Salvation Army guy there before, especially at night, and he seemed to be using a set of keys instead of a bell to invoke the Christmas spirit. Somebody checks it out—hell, they have a command center over on Grace, not three blocks from where the guy was standing—and they find out that he's a freelancer who figured a way to make a little extra Christmas money appealing to people's goodwill. A couple of shop owners beat the crap out of him, and now he wants to file charges for assault and robbery.

"Robbery?" Ray Long said over on the copy desk. "Jesus Christ. It's like killing your parents and asking for mercy because you're an orphan."

Well, times are tough, no matter what the president says. Lots of people are going beyond the pale to afford that extra toy or pint. Every stoplight you hit has a hard-luck case staring you down, begging for dollars. I actually gave one of them two bucks today. He had sign that read "Crowdsourcing for me." He looked healthier than I do—yeah, a low bar—but I did appreciate the creativity, and he made me laugh. Plus, he spelled "crowdsourcing" right. And he didn't put "God Bless" on the bottom of the sign. Extra points for that.

There were two shootings on the South Side, both of them about drugs, neither of them fatal. The shootings made the briefs. We put the bogus Salvation Army guy in a box on B1. A little seasonal levity, as Enos Jackson said.

Then, about eleven fifteen, I get a call. It's Peachy.

"I think I might have something," she says.

There was a cop who just retired, she tells me. He wasn't happy about his "retirement," which came a couple of months after a teenage kid in his custody somehow managed to beat himself severely about the head and shoulders. On the heels of some other unfortunate incidents elsewhere involving our men in blue, in addition to Walker Gunderson's somewhat tainted history, it was in everyone's best interests if Gunderson left the force. Offered the chance to plea to something that only put him on probation, he reluctantly agreed that it was time to go.

"Gunner Gunderson?"

"The same."

Yeah, we wrote something at the time, maybe four months ago, about the kid's family raising hell. They felt that their son, no paragon of virtue, probably didn't deserve a pretrial beatdown by the guy who arrested him. The police department stonewalled us. Even Peachy kept quiet on that one. But I had the impression there was some kind of settlement, and Gunner Gunderson quietly disappeared.

I knew him slightly from my first stint on night cops, back in the eighties. He always reminded me of a Nazi extra in a World War II movie, with that short blond hair and square face. He didn't take a lot of crap from suspected criminals back then. I guess he didn't mellow with age.

"He was pretty pissed, said they threw him under the bus," Peachy says. "I think if anybody would be willing to tell you something just because the chief didn't want him to, it would be Gunderson."

She has his address. He's living in one of the apartments they've hacked out of the old John Marshall Hotel downtown. Those things don't come cheap, so I gather Gunner got to keep his pension.

The John Marshall is across Franklin Street from Penny Lane, an easy nine-iron from my desk in the newsroom. I wonder if I might buy Gunderson a drink and mix business with pleasure. I tell Peachy I'll call him tomorrow and promise to call her again soon too.

Sometimes I feel bad for using Peachy. I'd feel worse if she didn't have a regular boyfriend who stays over about as often as Peachy will let him. As is the case with so many human transactions, we use each other.

I'M GETTING ready to call it a night, more than happy to head straight for my bed after a fourteen-hour day for which I'll get paid for eight, when I get a call on my cell phone. It is always a good idea, with post-midnight calls where you don't recognize the number, to let whoever's on the other end leave a message.

But I can't help myself. Andi says it's generational. My geezer peers and I consider it a mortal damn sin not to answer a ringing, beeping, or, in my case, blues-playing phone.

I'm immediately sorry I did.

"That you, Willie?"

I recognize Big Boy Sunday's voice. He sounds like he's got his mouth full. Maybe he's inhaling that "fourth meal" one of the fast-food chains keeps telling me we Americans need, seeing as how we're so skinny and malnourished.

I tell him that it is me, and that I'm just about to head out the door. I'm hoping he'll get the hint. He doesn't.

"How's it going?" he says. I'm pretty sure he's not inquiring about my general well-being.

I'm not about to tell Big Boy everything I know, unless one of his goons is holding an Uzi to my head. I tell him that I'm still digging, still trying to find some way to get McNish off the hook.

"Sounds like they're coming down pretty hard on the man, trying to set fire to his church and all."

I note that it seems like the neighbors never wanted Grace of God there in the first place.

Big Boy laughs.

"Yeah. It brings in the wrong element, know what I mean? How come you're not writin' anything about all this mess?"

I explain that I'm kind of tied up with the other big murder we're using to sell papers.

"Oh, yeah. That guy."

It seems unlikely, but I ask.

"You know him? Alderman?"

He takes a few seconds to either finish off his bedtime snack or think.

"I know of him," he says at last.

"Ever hear anything about him, I mean anything bad?"

"Now why would I be privy to anything about a fine, upstanding man like that? I'm surprised at you, Willie. What are you implying?"

I tell him that, if he does hear anything, I'd appreciate it if he'd pass it on.

"Man," Big Boy says, "you got a suspicious mind, Willie."

I tell him that I expect to be writing something about the McNish murder again sometime soon. This is somewhat wishful thinking. I am pretty sure that our publisher wants me to focus my attention on James Alderman for the foreseeable future. An e-mail from Wheelie earlier today reinforced that suspicion.

"Well, I certainly hope so," he says. "We want to see some justice around here."

If the legal system's version of justice had been applied, I want to tell Big Boy, he'd have been a guest of the state a long time ago for more than just a couple of years. But some things are best left unsaid.

Before he hangs up, he asks me a strange question.

"Do you think the cops have given Alderman's house a good going-over?"

"No idea. Why?"

"Oh, nothing. Just thought they'd be searching that place with a fine-tooth comb, him being such a big shot and all."

I tell Big Boy I'll ask, but that I'm not getting a lot of cooperation from the authorities these days.

"Well," he says, "I know you'll find a way, Willie. I'm counting on you."

It is somewhat disturbing to me that I could be in danger of disappointing Big Boy Sunday, who seems used to getting his way.

CHAPTER THIRTEEN

Wednesday

I wait until after nine to call Gunner Gunderson. Still, I have the impression I woke him up. It doesn't seem to cut any ice with him that we might have spoken to each other once or twice a quarter-century ago.

When I start asking about James Alderman, he informs me that since he isn't a cop anymore, he really doesn't give a rat's ass about who gets killed and who doesn't.

"These people," he says. "They want law and order, but they don't want to do what it takes, you know?"

I exude heartfelt sympathy. I concede that perhaps our newspaper was a little hard on him. We did have an editorial that took a strong stand on police brutality after his career-ending faux pas. When I point out that I don't write the editorials, it didn't fly. It seldom does.

"All you bastards," Gunderson says, "you're all alike. You never get the cops' side of the story."

I think I do, but now's not the time to let pride fuck up a good source.

When I'm finally able to get the gun turned toward the police department hierarchy rather than the paper, my prospects of having a sit-down get a little more promising.

He rants a bit about what these other bastards, most especially Chief L.D. Jones, did to him. I make sympathetic noises and let him vent.

When he stops to catch his breath, I get to the reason for my call.

"There was a case, a long time ago, where I think the facts might have been covered up. It had to do with James Alderman. You were on the street back then. I thought you might know something about it."

He seems to take the bait, but he's still just nibbling, wanting to know why I'm digging up crap from way back then.

I explain that we're just acting on a story we heard, that might or might not be true. I mention that what I'm trying to find could be embarrassing to the department.

I hear him cough and spit.

I ask him if we can talk, maybe at Penny Lane.

"Nah," he says. "I'll meet you at the pool hall. The one on Sixth Street, right around the corner."

Sounds good to me.

"What we're talking about," he says, "it's got to be off the record, right?"

I tell him anything I use will be not for attribution. I'll use it, but I won't say who said it.

"OK," he says. "But you better not screw me on this. I don't think I'm supposed to be talking to anybody about anything these days. Don't want to mess up my pension."

We agree to meet at three. Alderman's funeral is at one. I call and leave a message to let Sally Velez know I'll be a little late coming in today.

I'M SUPPOSED to meet McGonnigal and Andy Peroni for coffee over at the place on Main at ten. I get there a few minutes late.

Normally this would be a treat. Not today. Not after the breaking off of relations with Cindy. I'm half ashamed for what I did, and I'm a little pissed at Andy for not somehow pleading my case more eloquently, as I lay passed out on that Williamsburg Lodge bed with puke drying on my shirt.

I asked Andy if he still wanted to meet today. Custalow couldn't get away from his duties at the Prestwould. Maybe we could reschedule? Like maybe 2017?

"Now more than ever," Andy says. "Friends don't let friends weasel out of social events just because they fucked up."

Well, at least he didn't say we "need to talk." Please, God, don't make this an intervention.

When I get there, there is, as expected, no mercy.

"I understand they're thinking about putting a histori-cal marker in the Regency Room," McGonnigal says before I've even gotten my coffee. "'On this spot, on December 14, 2014, Willie Mays Black suffered a one-round knockout, the most decisive setback of his pugilistic career.' Nice shiner, by the way."

One thing I can say for my oldest friends: With the exception of Custalow, who tries to never speak ill of anyone, they don't pull their punches. Fuck-ups don't fester among my Oregon Hill pals. They are trotted out into the sunlight in all their shining glory, over and over. I'm just glad Goat Johnson isn't here to triple-team me.

I remind McGonnigal of a few of his more egregious sins. Unlike him, I have never driven home after a hearty night of partying, walked into the house, gone to sleep, and realized the next morning that the car was out of gas because no one bothered to turn off the ignition the night before.

I remind Andy of the time his then-girlfriend called his home number rather than his cell number by mistake and left a two-minute phone sex message, which was instrumental in Andy's wife at the time throwing him out of the house for a couple of weeks and later sending him a phone sex message of her own, apparently while in the throes of extramarital bliss.

"Yeah," Andy says, "she's never told me who it was, either."

"Well," R.P. says, "I think you can rule me out. I'd already switched sides by then."

"Wasn't me," I add. "That only leaves about one hundred thousand other guys in the city, plus a few hundred thousand in the suburbs. I'm sure you'll figure it out eventually."

We continue to play "how low can you go?" for a few minutes more, getting the occasional strange glance from the hipsters and college kids around us. Fuck 'em. We've been having coffee and telling stories on each other since before a lot of these assholes were born. This is our side of town, and we don't lower our voices for anybody.

I ask Andy, on the way out, if he thinks there's any way I haven't permanently screwed the pooch with Cindy.

"I don't know, Willie. She was pretty upset. I've seen her get pissed off lots of times. She'll throw a tantrum and then she'll be over it. The sun comes out.

"This was different, though. She just seemed sad."

There's a lot of that going around. If I stop and think about how bad I've messed up, I might have to go somewhere dark and sedate myself.

"Do you think I should call her?"

Andy stops in front of his car and faces me.

"I don't know. I really don't know. Goddammit, Willie, there is nothing I'd rather see than you and my baby sister walking down the aisle someday, even if you're so old you

need a walker. But she's a little leery right now, not quite sure
what she's signed on for, you know?"

I nod my head and thank my old friend. Not much else
to do. Maybe I'll try to call her tomorrow. "Try" as in try to
get up the nerve.

꒳

THEY'VE AGREED to have the services at Saint Paul's, Alderman's career worshipping a Presbyterian god notwithstanding.
So many of his social and clerical friends and associates are
Episcopalian, and Saint Paul's is where the really big wheels
get their going-away parties.

The place is packed, as I knew it would be. I park three
blocks away on Grace and hope I've put enough time on the
meter.

James Alderman didn't have any family to speak of, it
appears. He has a brother, a few years younger, who is supposed to be some kind of old-money mover and shaker. A
couple of cousins, one of them quite elderly, also are in attendance. But he seemed to have touched just about every part
of the city. The university and civic leaders and a variety of
church-related people are among the throng. I recognize a
couple of former mayors and half a dozen city council members, past and present.

The service is serviceable, but I can't help wishing that
they could have done it at one of the African American
churches, or at least imported the choir from one of them.
I can still remember the funeral, last year, of Philomena's
younger brother. The guy dropped dead from a heart attack at
sixty-two. He ran a car-repair shop and probably had a high
school education, but the funeral went over two hours and
was highlighted by the kind of wailing and gnashing of teeth
that I hope will be in evidence when I shuffle off.

Of course, if the Episcopalians had that kind of service, I'd never be able to make my three o'clock appointment with Gunner Gunderson.

The minister says all the right things, although without enough heat to warm up this bleak December day. I see Clara Westbrook and a couple of other Prestwouldians among the attendees.

I get a few quotes from some of the notables to go with my story for tomorrow's paper. By 2:40, I'm on the street, getting in a quick smoke before I get back to my car. When I get there, of course, there's a ticket on it. My goddamn third one this month. Apparently the meter maids don't have a bereavement policy.

There is a silver lining in the crap storm though. In a small bit of serendipity, I've parked so far west of Saint Paul's that it's easy to walk from the car to Sixth Street. I am able to persuade the guy in the half-ass convenience store to grudgingly give me two dollars in change so my ticket doesn't have a buddy by the time I get back. I've probably bought a couple of thousand dollars in cigarettes off this guy, but today I'm a stranger. Maybe it's the tie.

They've just opened the pool hall here. It takes up a space on the ground floor of the John Marshall's back side. The hotel's rebirth gives me hope for our hard-pressed city. It was a grand old place for decades, gradually slipping into squalor toward the end. The state press association had its annual awards banquets there every couple of years or so. Half the newspaper people in the state would come, since being a print journalist at awards time is like being on a youth soccer team. Everybody gets a damn trophy.

In my earlier days at the paper, they'd spring for free rooms here on snow nights. Any staffers who didn't feel safe driving home in a blizzard got to stay at the John Marshall and charge their meals. And blizzards were interpreted very loosely—anything over five inches usually did the trick. More than once, a bunch of us would stay up half the night, playing poker and drinking the cheap booze we'd stocked up on at the ABC store next to the paper. We'd order room service, then manage to get breakfast and lunch on the tab before we came back to work the next afternoon. These days, if you don't feel safe driving home, you need to bring a sleeping bag. That newsroom floor is pretty hard.

Then, sometime in the late eighties, when cities were on life-support, it closed. Every three or four years, somebody with a big hat and damn few cattle would announce a plan to bring it back. They'd make a little noise, show everyone a lot of pretty "artist's renderings," and then disappear.

Finally somebody walked the walk. Instead of imploding the place and building another damn parking deck, we've saved something worth saving.

I'm a couple of minutes late. I spot Gunderson immediately, at one of the back tables next to Franklin Street. Other than the blond hair turning gray, he doesn't seem to have changed much. The guy at the front counter says Gunner told him I'd be paying, so I guess I am.

I like the place. I've been in a couple of times with Custalow, and once with Cindy, who has a pretty good touch with a pool cue. They don't have flat-screen TVs, so it isn't a sports bar with pool tables. They have banners with the likeness of people like Wimpy Lassiter on them. The place is about shooting pool, but it isn't a joint where people sometimes use the cue sticks to beat the crap out of each other. I guess the high-end beer keeps the riffraff out. It's the kind of place where guys with their own sticks in leather cases play by themselves next to couples on dates.

I introduce myself.

"I know who you are," Gunderson says, the way you might say it to a child molester. He doesn't bother to look up from the shot he's about to miss. "You're the guy that brought Shiflett down."

Yeah, I did. Five years ago. No apologies for that. A guy cuts a girl's head off and mails it to her father, he probably needs nailing, even if he is a lieutenant.

I tell him what I'm after. I mention the kind of hoo-ha that could erupt if what I suspect is true.

"Get a stick," he says, and we proceed to play a couple of games of eight ball. I order a five-dollar beer with a cute name that tastes about half as good as a Miller.

I don't push him. He knows what I want, and he'll only give it to me if it suits him.

About the time I'm losing the first game by sinking the cue ball along with the eight, he starts talking.

"They wanted it to disappear," he says, "so it disappeared."

He wasn't the cop who responded when the kid's mother called the police. But he was there when they went to Alderman's house to question him.

"Ordinarily, they'd have hauled his ass down to the station, tried to sweat it out of him," Gunderson says. "But this guy, they gave him the velvet-glove treatment. He seemed nervous. I guess he knew that kid might be able to identify him. Hell, as I remember it, he didn't live but four or five blocks away."

I rack 'em. Gunderson breaks and keeps talking.

"The detective who showed the kid the pictures told us he picked out this guy Alderman right away."

He sinks two balls before he misses.

"But they never did bring Alderman in."

I ask him when the kid changed his story.

"It wasn't long, maybe two or three days. In the meantime, we were told in no uncertain terms that this wasn't going to

get out, that we weren't going to malign somebody who might
be innocent."

He laughs, upsetting my concentration.

"Like we gave a shit on a normal day."

I ask him if he was there when the kid recanted.

"No, but I know somebody who was."

He goes silent, grinning and busting my chops, making
me beg for it.

"Who?"

"The big dog. The lord high emperor of us all."

Jesus H. Christ. It's possible. L.D. Jones would have been
on the force about five years by then, still trying to make his
bones.

Gunderson insists that he knows for a fact that the chief
was there, because he told Gunderson and a couple of other
cops about it over beers.

"He said the kid seemed like he was scared, and his
mother did most of the talking. But even when they threatened to send his bony ass to jail for making false charges and
wasting our fucking time, he stuck with the story. His mother
was right there beside him, L.D. said, and she was more sure
than the kid that he'd picked the wrong guy.

"But there never was any right guy. Kid didn't see anyone
else who looked like he might have wanted to use him for his
play toy.

"So, it just died."

I drop the thirteen ball in the far corner pocket and then
sink the twelve in the side, a ninety-degree shot I make about
once a year. Gunderson calls me a lucky SOB, and he's right,
but I pretend it's just business as usual.

L.D. Jones has got some 'splainin' to do. In the meantime,
though, there is one piece of information that is going to

make my time with the charming Gunner Gunderson worth it, even if I do get stuck with the bill for pool time and the beer.

No sense in pussyfooting around it.

"Do you know who the kid was?"

Gunderson grins.

"Yeah," he says. "I figured you'd be asking that, sooner or later."

He reaches into his pocket and pulls out a piece of paper.

"The cop who answered the call, he retired about six years ago, but I called him. He's got a good memory. And he kept pretty good records, on his own. Said he was going to write one of them police books, like *Onion Field*, you know. But he never did. Shit, the guy couldn't write his name."

I look at the name the other retired cop gave Gunderson, and the address. It's twenty years old, but it's a start.

To ease my pain a little at pay-up time, I sink the eight ball this time without scratching.

"Don't be a stranger," I say to Gunderson as he leaves.

He extends his middle finger by way of acknowledgment.

I STOP by and ask Sally if she thinks I'll be able to write off three beers and an hour of pool as a business expense. She urges me to try it. She says she'd like to watch.

I write the funeral story. As those things go, I think it's pretty good. Enos Jackson says I have a real future as an obit writer.

Sarah has been working the McNish beat, but she's not getting anywhere. Nobody seems to have seen Artesian Cole after he left Grace of God.

I call her into one of the conference rooms and fill her in on what I've just learned from Gunderson.

"Damn," she says. "Willie, this is your story now. Who-ever writes this one, though, there's going to be a shit storm up in Suitville."

I assure her that I will need plenty of help, and I remind her that she was the one who ferreted out Stella Barnes.

"You've got rights on this one," I tell her. "Ask yourself, WWBD. What would Baer do?"

Mark Baer, still hoping to climb above our humble rag and into his rightful place in the journalism pantheon, some-times uses his coworkers' heads for stepping-stones. He is on the bad side of some of said coworkers right now. He has lob-bied to get his name added to an investigative reporting entry in the state press contest. Sarah and another reporter did 99 percent of the work. Baer, it turned out, gave Sarah a couple of phone numbers she needed. But when they hand out those résumé-enhancing two-dollar plaques, Baer's will be just as big as Sarah's.

"Fuck Baer," Sarah says. Since they are not dating any-more, I optimistically take this to be figurative rather than literal.

I call Kate at home to see how McNish is doing. She says that she and Marcus have little hope of getting the judge to set bail, which means he can expect to be in the lockup for a bit longer.

"Unless the cops find something they haven't found already, like somebody who saw the boy that afternoon with some-body other than our client."

She asks me if I'm still on the story.

"Not officially."

"Which means you are."

"Now that James Alderman is underground, maybe they'll let me get back on it."

I hear her sigh.

"You're not telling me everything, are you, Willie?"

I can't think of anything better to say, just before hanging up, than, "Did I ever?"

Sarah's main contribution to tomorrow's paper will be the revelation that the black community (with, it is hoped, a few white contributors) is planning a protest. Nothing radical like what went on in that town in Missouri when the unarmed black guy got aired out by the police, of course. Richmond is, as one of our veteran cynics says, a hotbed of rest, and they do have a pretty good excuse for a suspect down in the city lockup. But people concerned about perspective want to do something to let the police know that the disappearance of those young African American boys is just as worthy of justice as the murder of a James Alderman.

L.D. Jones is no doubt feeling the heat. I almost feel sorry for him. Not sorry enough, however, to pass on confronting him about a meeting that did or didn't take place two decades ago.

CHAPTER FOURTEEN

Thursday

The demonstration doesn't amount to much. We are assured that peace without justice is like barbecue without coleslaw. The rally is held in front of city hall and manages to tie up traffic on Broad Street for a while. The organizers were wise enough to invite all the TV stations, though, and they'll have some nice footage for the noon and evening news. Clever camera angles can make the eighty or so attendees look like a few hundred. The mayor and the chief both assure their viewing audience that they will bring all their considerable powers to bear to ensure that the perpetrator of this heinous crime pays the price. The mayor pronounces it "hee-in-us." L.D. looks tired. His bodyguard and the mayor's protection stand behind them scowling.

Sarah's covering for us, but I go over anyhow, hoping to catch the chief for a brief chat afterward.

His bodyguard tries to shoo me away, and he certainly has the arms to do it. When I talk over the goon, though, and tell L.D. I've spoken with someone about a certain meeting twenty years ago, a meeting that involved James Alderman, I know I've winged him from the way he breaks stride. We're out of range of the TV folks. I hope the chief appreciates my discretion.

"Come by after two," is all he says as he scurries away.

SOME THINGS can't be put off forever.

Today's the day I put on my big boy pants and seek Cindy Peroni's forgiveness. The worst scenario, I think, will be if she forgives me but tells me I'm just too much damn trouble. That'll mean that the L-word, the one we've both said to each other on occasion, is out of the picture. You're either in it or you're not.

If she's only furious with me, I might have a chance. Right now, I'd be glad to let her club me with a nine iron just to know she cares.

I make the call at eleven thirty, half hoping she'll be out Christmas shopping. She's finished her classes for the semester, and her part-time job is mostly nights.

She answers. I almost hang up. Despite grinding my teeth over this since Monday, I can't think of a damn thing to say.

"Um, hi, it's me. The asshole."

She is silent for a few long seconds.

"Hello, Willie."

I strain in vain to hear anything resembling warmth.

I tell her how sorry I am, in both senses: regretful as hell and worthless as a broke-dick dog. I explain how ashamed I am, how I never in a million years meant for last Sunday's disaster to happen. I explain that I would rather take poison, or even go to the ballet, than hurt her.

There's no sound coming from the other end of the line, and I am concerned for a second that she has quietly hung up the phone. But I hear breathing. She's waiting me out, doing what I do when I want a subject to spill his guts. Damn, I taught her that.

She lets me finish making my case.

"I know I don't deserve anything, and I know you've told me before what the consequences are, so I can't do anything but beg you. Please forgive me. Please take me back."

I hear her snort.

"You son of a bitch," she says for openers, then spends the next couple of minutes telling me exactly how many fathoms lower than whale shit I am. Now it's time for me to shut up.

"I hate you," she says, winding up.

It's crunch time.

"But do you love me?"

She doesn't answer right away. I am outside, in the parking lot beside the Prestwould. I throw down the Camel I'm holding in my left hand and cross my fingers.

"I don't know," she says at last. "Oh, hell, I can't lie. I do. But that just makes it worse."

"Yeah. I know."

"You're going to have to give me some time, Willie. I appreciate that you didn't promise it'll never happen again. It will, unless you get some help or just grow the hell up.

"It's just a question of whether I can put up with a drunk who is liable to ruin everything on a moment's notice."

"A guy who could fuck up Christmas."

"Yeah. That guy."

I note that, in my defense, I'm not drunk all the time. We both knew men and women, in Oregon Hill, who started drinking when they woke up and stopped when they passed out. I was luckier than many. Peggy's mind-altering substance of choice only made her mellow and a little goofy.

"Is it OK if I call you in a few days?"

She says maybe, but then she says it'd be better if she calls me.

"I promise I won't leave you hanging," she says, "but I sure as hell can't swear that you're going to like the answer."

It's all I can hope for and more than I deserve.

THE LONG-AGO boy's name isn't listed in the white pages. It's not on switchboard.com or anywhere else I look. Hell, maybe he's dead.

I make a call to Philomena Slade, because Philomena seems to know everybody. She is pretty much one degree of separation from any African American in the greater Richmond area.

I tell her I'm trying to find a man named Alston Barefoot, who would be about thirty-two now, if I'm doing the math right.

"What do you want to talk to him for?" she asks me. Even if I am family, she has a fact-based suspicion of anybody wearing a tie who's looking for a black man. I'm not a bill collector and I'm not serving a warrant, but my being a journalist is enough to make my cousin suspicious.

I tell her that he might have some information that could help solve Artesian Cole's murder.

Appeased, she spills it.

"Lord have mercy," she says. "I think I knew who he is. I believe I went to school with his momma. They're good people. Surely to goodness he isn't involved in this mess."

I assure Momma Phil that Alston Barefoot isn't guilty of anything other than maybe not telling the truth twenty years ago.

Philomena doesn't know where Alston Barefoot's mother lives now, but she's pretty sure she's around Richmond somewhere.

"Can you find out where her son lives?"

She hesitates. I hate to ask her, but the chances of this guy's mother giving some stranger her son's address are about the same as the Redskins winning next year's Super Bowl. Maybe she'll grant special dispensation to an old schoolmate.

Finally she says she'll see what she can do. I assure her that nothing bad is going to happen to Mr. Barefoot, wherever he is.

To SAY that L.D. Jones is not happy to see me would be a gross understatement. It is obvious that he's receiving me because he's got no damn choice.

"I don't have much time," he says, glancing at his watch. "I've gotta be somewhere in fifteen minutes. Say what you come to say."

The chief looks a tad frazzled. He's got one man locked up for murdering a kid and is feeling the heat to tack every missing African American boy over the last two decades to Sam McNish's hapless carcass. In the meantime, his doughty forces haven't made much progress in figuring out who slaughtered one of the city's most beloved citizens.

So I lay it out for him. I hate making L.D.'s day a little longer than it is already, but sometimes you have to hit him upside the head with a two-by-four to get his attention. And, like many of the powerful individuals I have to deal with on a professional basis, he would rather undergo a colonoscopy without anesthesia than admit that he's wrong.

If it is possible for a man of the chief's hue to turn red, he has done so.

"Where," he asks me, "did you get that shit?"

"You know I can't tell you who told me, but you know I wouldn't be here if I didn't believe it."

"Bullshit. You just want something to print. You don't care who you hurt."

I try to reassure L.D. that I'm not out to get him, that I don't even plan to run his name. After a lot of harsh words on his part and placating ones on mine, his temperature lowers to a slow simmer.

"I just need a little confirmation," I tell him. "That's all."

He scratches his head, which is almost as bald as mine. He sighs.

"It was a long time ago," the chief says.

L.D. Jones was just three years on the force when Alston Barefoot and his mother sat down with him and two other cops and told them that he had been mistaken in identifying James Alderman as the man who tried to drag him into his car.

"He acted like he didn't really want to be there, and his mother kept after him, like 'Go on, go on.'

"We didn't think much of the whole thing. It seemed like the kid was a puppet, you know, with Momma pulling the strings."

But young Alston continued to recant his earlier identification. Even the threat of jail for making a false accusation didn't sway him.

"We still wanted to go after it," the chief says. "But then my lieutenant, a big old mean redneck named Creed, called me in. He told me that if I wanted a career in law enforcement, I'd be advised to believe the boy and go on about my business.

"And so I did."

The boy wasn't able to identify anybody else, either, and the alleged crime fell into a black hole.

I wonder out loud if any of this rang a bell when Alderman was recently butchered.

He hesitates, then nods his head.

"Yeah. But that was a one-and-done. If the man did anything wrong twenty years ago, he wasn't convicted. And he sure as hell hasn't been convicted of anything since then, if you ignore a speeding ticket twelve years ago."

"So you did check up."

He glares at me.

"I'm not an idiot. I always check up. I just don't call your ass every time I do."

Fair enough. But something else occurs to me.

"L.D, I know you can't tell me, but if there's anybody out there now leaning on you to back off the late Mr. Alderman, I'm going to make it easy on you. I'm going to get up and leave now. If you're getting heat from higher up, don't say anything."

A variation of an old Woodward and Bernstein trick, although it kind of backfired on them. Still, I've used it to good advantage more than once.

I get up, turn, and head toward the door. I even hesitate for a couple of seconds before walking out. The chief doesn't say a word.

THERE ARE maybe thirty people in the newsroom when I get back, a pretty good turnout for a Thursday afternoon. I see half a dozen of my coworkers standing by a table halfway across the room. They seem amused.

The building was rebuilt from the ground up a few years before people stopped reading newspapers, and they left room for about three times the staff we have now. The table, which I see holds a fake, butt-ugly Christmas tree, is a good twenty feet from the nearest desk. Lots of wide-open spaces in print journalism these days.

As I get closer, I see that the tree has been decorated, after a fashion. There are a couple of dozen plastic cards taped to the faux tree. They are all twenty-five-dollar gift certificates to Food Lion. Chuck Apple explains that they're going to take them all down and give them to the needy on Christmas Eve. For now, they are making a statement to whoever signs the checks. The statement begins with "fuck" and ends with "you."

I am sure that Rita Dominick is not going to be pleased, but she probably doesn't want to be seen as the kind of publisher who can't take a little joke. That's my guess, because otherwise she'd have already ordered Wheelie to take it down.

There's an e-mail waiting for me when I get back to my desk. It is from the aforementioned Ms. Dominick. It is tightly written: See Me.

I am assuming that she is not calling me to the suit floor to give me a raise. I give Sandy McCool my best "what the fuck?" look as I head for the top lady's office. Sandy gives me her best "hell if I know" shrug.

The publisher is on the phone and nods for me to take a seat. She is all sweetness and light, laughing at some off-color remark and cooing, "Now, Scott, you know you shouldn't be saying things like that. I could bring you up for sexual harassment." Must be an advertiser. I am convinced that Rita Dominick would perform oral sex on anybody who was willing to buy a full-page ad at full price. Hell, she probably already has. The way things are going, the whole newsroom might need kneepads soon.

As soon as she hangs up, the sweetness and light are replaced by a decidedly sour darkness.

"I hear you're looking into James Alderman," she says.

I tell her that is my present assignment.

"You know what I mean," she says. "You're digging into things that happened, what, twenty years ago? Things that never led to criminal charges."

Amazing. Goddamn L.D. must have called somebody up his own personal food chain, who must have called the publisher. Is this a small town or what?

"Let me follow this up. I'm close to getting . . ."

"You're close to getting fired. Anything you write about James Alderman damn well better be a nomination for sainthood."

I don't like getting interrupted. I don't like money-grubbing assholes turning journalists into whores who do the bidding of the comfortable. It is obvious to me that Alderman, despite the lack of heartfelt emotion at his funeral services, has some strong advocates. Or maybe it's just that the movers and shakers don't want the embarrassment of having one of their own pulled down off the pedestal.

Still, if I have any hope of finding out if my hunch is true, I do have to avoid the annoyance of being fired. I can't afford to buy my own printing press.

She lectures me a bit more on the inappropriateness of disrespecting the dead. I promise, with fingers firmly crossed inside my pants pocket, to be a good boy and play nice.

Rita Dominick can kiss my ass if she thinks I'm backing off this one.

"And you're probably behind that goddamn Christmas tree too," she says as I exit.

I don't disabuse her.

WHEN I get back downstairs, properly chastened, there are no homicides to merit my attention. I'm playing solitaire on my computer when Philomena Slade calls.

She tells me why I couldn't find Alston Barefoot.

"His momma died a couple of years ago," Philomena says. "Another girl we went to school with told me. She'd moved to Newport News. I expect that's why I didn't know about it. They must of not put an obituary in the paper, or I would of seen it."

This doesn't sound promising, but she adds, "Her sister, though, she was a couple of years ahead of me in school, she was able to tell me what you wanted."

It turns out that Alston Barefoot is neither these days. At some point after his encounter with James Alderman, he took his stepfather's last name, and he started calling himself by his middle name. Ray Soles. Ray-Ray to his friends, my cousin tells me.

I'm wondering whether I can track down Mr. Soles. Philomena saves me the trouble. She reads off an address over on the North Side, east of Chamberlayne and not too far from where the late James Alderman lived and died.

I thank her profusely and promise to drop by and give her a big kiss at the next opportunity.

"Just remember what you promised," she says. "Nothing bad better happen to that boy."

I promise again. I don't want Ray-Ray Soles. I want information.

Sally gives me permission to leave my post for a couple of hours, with the caveat that she will call me if any of our citizens do notable harm to each other. She doesn't even have to be told to cover for me in case our publisher wants to know where the night cops reporter is. She knows I wouldn't slip away just to have a couple of beers. Well, probably not.

I find the address, off North Avenue in Highland Park. It's six o'clock, already long past dark, by the time I get there. Philomena told me he's a mailman.

A light is on in what looks like the living room. I stub my Camel, go to the door, and knock, hoping I don't look too much like a bill collector.

I see someone peek out through the curtains. I wait. I think for a while nobody's going to answer the door—a reasonable reaction in this neighborhood when somebody you don't know comes knocking after sundown.

Then it opens with the chain still attached.

"What you want?" a voice on the other side asks.

I explain as quickly and unthreateningly as I can that I am from the newspaper and that James Alderman's murder unearthed some records about an accusation made against him two decades ago. He starts to slam the door shut. I wedge my size twelve into the opening and try to convince him that he is in no danger of being prosecuted, or even identified.

"I'm not the police," I explain. "I'm just a guy whose boss wants him to try and find out what happened back then. Help a brother out."

"Brother" is a shameless stretch, but maybe he can see that we are at least nominally linked by race. Or maybe the truth, as persistent as water in finding a weak spot, has been pent up for too long.

He opens the door. I make the same promise I seem to have been making all day today: No names. I just need information.

"Dammit," he says, when we're seated on the Naugahyde couch, "I knew, when I saw that that man got killed, I knew this was going to come back."

And so, Ray-Ray Soles, thirty-two and divorced, with two kids living with his ex-wife, his feet aching from delivering

Christmas shit all day long, puts his sore tootsies on the ottoman and tells me what really happened twenty years ago.

"I came home from school two days after I identified the guy, and my momma was sitting in the living room. I knew something was wrong, because she never waited for me like that. Normally, she'd have been scrambling around, getting ready for work. She was working in maintenance over at MCV, the hospital, and she was on the late shift.

"I was afraid something had happened to my stepfather."

It was less dire and more complicated, though. A man, "some white guy, she didn't even know what he looked like; they all kind of looked alike to her," had come calling while her son was at school.

He had in his possession a check for ten thousand dollars, made out to her.

"My memory was it looked like it was from some corporation or something. Didn't really matter. It was ten thousand dollars."

The tradeoff, of course, was retroactive amnesia. The future Ray-Ray Soles was supposed to tell the police he had made a mistake. The man he identified as his would-be assailant wasn't the man after all.

Soles shakes his head.

"It didn't even matter that much to me at the time. Ten thousand paid off the mortgage. It let Momma take a job making a little less money but working day hours."

He points to a photograph of his mother, framed over the TV set.

"But it bothered her every day. She knew it wasn't right. But people that are always 'doing the right thing' don't understand how hard it is to do right when you can't pay the bills."

He sighs.

"And, yeah, it bothers me, too, now that I can think about it. What if this had something to do with those other boys disappearing? I mean, when a kid would turn up missing, I'd read about it and wonder.

"When I'd hear the kids talking about 'Frosty,' I'd wonder, was that Frosty?

"But he never showed up again, except when he'd get elected to something or other or get some big award. So I thought, that can't be the guy.

"Now, I don't know. I'm just glad he's gone, I guess."

There is one more question that needs answering.

"Are you absolutely sure that the guy who tried to grab you was James Alderman?"

He looks me square in the eye and takes his sore feet off the ottoman.

"As sure as I'm sittin' here."

CHAPTER FIFTEEN

Friday

I called Kate last night. It didn't seem that late to me, sometime shortly after nine. As I was informed, though, it was late for a mother with a nearly two-year-old who has her mom's energy level and a newfound vocabulary that reportedly consists mostly of "No."

She accepted my apologies after she completely woke up though. I told her it was time to put a little more heat on the police, encouraging them to reconsider holding Sam McNish for one or multiple murders of young boys. I explained why.

"Holy shit!" she said, and I could hear bedsprings squeaking and Mr. Ellis groaning in the background. Apparently, when the kid goes down at Chez Ellis, everybody goes down. I vaguely remember those nights, before I deserted Jeanette and Andi.

I make it clear to Kate that neither she nor Marcus Green will ever know the source of my information. All she needs to know is that it's accurate. Somehow, I told her, we have to convince L.D. Jones that he probably is barking up the wrong tree. I mention that I might be able to nudge him a little on that front as well.

"Maybe we can at least convince a judge to set bail, if the chief expresses some doubts."

"Persuade."

"What?"

"You persuade somebody to do something. You convince somebody of something."

Maybe it wasn't exactly the right time for a language usage lesson, but, goddamn, she's a lawyer. She advised me to have sex with myself and said she'd call me in the morning.

AND so she does. At six thirty.

"Hey," she says, all bright and chirpy, "I'm wide awake. Been up for an hour. Grace is an early riser. I hope you weren't still sleeping."

Touché.

She suggests that we get in touch with the chief as soon as possible. I tell her to let me handle it. I know L.D. gets in his office by eight thirty. That'll give me an hour or so to sleep.

At 8:35, I call. It is a positive sign that I am transferred to the chief right away. After yesterday's conversation, I apparently have his ear.

I explain that I can, if necessary, produce rather compelling evidence that the boy who identified James Alderman all those years ago was bought off. I explain that I have found the boy, now a grown man. I don't have to explain that I know L.D. was there when all this was going down, and how big a turd this could leave at his doorstep.

"Bullshit," he says, but I can tell from the tone of his voice that he knows he's got trouble.

He wants a name. I tell him that isn't possible. I figure that nothing the present Ray-Ray Soles did under duress from his mother twenty years ago is actionable at this point, but I did promise.

I tell him that I'm sure Sam McNish's lawyers will be contacting him later today, urging him to rethink his prime suspect in Artesian Cole's murder.

He turns almost plaintive on me, something L.D. Jones does approximately every time they have frost in hell.

"Why are you doing this?" he asks. "Maybe we do need to take another look at this, but you can't think James Alderman had something to do with that boy's death."

I tell him that I don't know what to think right now. I ask him if he has any more leads on who might have dispatched Alderman.

He tells me it's an ongoing investigation. Some things never change.

I HAVE a rare Friday night off. Not really my choice. The only halfway generous perk for the newsroom anymore is vacation time. They haven't slashed that, probably because it doesn't hurt the bottom line. I still have four weeks a year. Unfortunately, it's more than I can use with good conscience. With the shrinking staff, taking a day off just means somebody else has to work twice as hard. But, faced with the prospect of giving away vacation time—it doesn't carry over—and given the opportunity to be there when my grandson gets his first googly-eyed gander at the Christmas lights at the Botanical Gardens, I stick poor Chuck Apple with Friday night cops. I'll make it up to him.

There are still four days I'll never get to use, unless Rita Dominick fires me before New Year's. The idea of giving up vacation time to the SOBs who make me punch in like a mill hand every day is almost too much to bear.

And yet, here I am, up and at 'em, working on my day off anyhow. And not just working, but working on a story that our esteemed publisher has told me to back the fuck away from.

It is a wonderful thing, I am told, to love your job. It would be more wonderful if it loved me back.

MARCUS GREEN arranges to talk with his client at eleven. I am invited to come along. Since whatever chance McNish has of being home for Christmas is mostly the result of what I've dug up, this seems reasonable.

Marcus drives Kate and me by Grace of God. The place is shut down. It would be anyhow, for the holidays, but this looks permanent. The graffiti is unoriginal and depressing. It appears that one of the windows has been broken out.

"I wonder if he'll ever get this thing back running again," Marcus says, "even if I do manage to get his ass off. Which I will."

I admit that it looks doubtful for Grace of God. The neighbors are trying to make sure the kids' after-school program never sees the light of day again. Their councilman is working hard to make sure the next owners of the rambling structure where Sam McNish was trying to save the world will be Lexus-driving yuppies, twenty- or thirty-somethings with plenty of money and no kids yet or people my age moving back into the city now that their offspring are out of school. Cool restaurants and hot nightlife are relatively easy for a city to bring in. Better schools? Good luck. The white folks took their kids and money to the suburbs long ago, and now they tsk-tsk and wonder why "those people" can't have good schools like the ones little Jacob and Elizabeth go to.

"Racist bastards," Marcus mutters, shocking me. He rarely lets his feelings surface on issues of color.

I remind him that Marcus Jr. is ensconced in one of the tonier high schools out in the 'burbs, a mile or so from the palatial estate Green was able to buy after becoming the city's best get-out-of-jail lawyer.

"Hey," he says, "white flight isn't just for white people anymore. It ain't about color anymore. What's my last name?"

OK. I'll play straight man.

"Green."

He nods his head.

"Yeah. Green. That's the color."

McNish seems serene. He has told me he does yoga. I wonder if that's sacrilege for a Presbyterian. Hell, if it can make a man in the Richmond city jail appear as at peace as he does now, maybe I need to buy myself a mat.

"There could be good news," Kate tells him. He nods and waits for it. She turns to me.

I explain that, while no one has been able to find anything that would absolve him of Artesian Cole's murder, no one has been able to find anything else that would pin it to him either, other than the word of a woman who seems to have been scorned by him.

And then I go into what I have found out about James Alderman.

For the first time, McNish seems disturbed.

"That is impossible," he says, leaning forward, jogged out of his personal nirvana. "You can't be thinking James Alderman had anything to do with any of this. He's the reason I chose the path I chose. The man is as close to a saint as you can get."

Nevertheless, I explain, the great man did apparently once try to abduct a young boy. Why, I ask McNish, would that boy, now grown, be willing to say that his original accusation of Alderman was accurate unless it was?

He shakes his head.

"I don't know. But even if he did do something like that all those years ago, what does that have to do with now?"

"You said he had spent time helping mentor the boys."

"Of course. But so did a lot of others."

I point out that none of the other mentors have, to our knowledge, ever been accused of attempting to abduct a young boy.

"We know you didn't do this," Kate says. "Can you give us any kind of information that might possibly point to James Alderman?"

He sits up straight in his chair. He looks like a kid who has just been given the goods about Santa Claus.

"This is wrong," he says. "If I had to go to prison for the rest of my life for a crime I didn't commit, I would never try to accuse James Alderman."

He won't budge. We are somewhat stunned, leaving the jail. We thought we were giving Sam McNish an early Christmas present, but he thinks we've left a steaming pile of crap on his doorstep.

"I don't know," Marcus says. "He's got his head up his ass so far I'm not sure we can extract it."

"He's loyal," I say. "He's got faith. He believes. In James Alderman."

Unfortunately, as we all know but don't say, faith doesn't have a lot of respect for facts.

Marcus shrugs his shoulders.

"Well, I guess we're gonna have to save his skinny ass in spite of himself."

Kate and Marcus drop me off at Perly's, where I am becoming fond, somehow, of the hot dog with a schmear of chopped chicken liver. A couple of other reporters are there, and it turns into a two-beer lunch.

It's a decent afternoon, considering we're two days shy of the shortest day of the year. The walk back to the Prestwould promises to be pleasant.

It becomes somewhat less so when a big-ass Explorer with tinted windows pulls up and a couple of guys I recognize from my last visit with Big Boy Sunday hop out and usher me inside.

It happens so fast. I am within eyesight of the police station on Grace, and there are people, albeit most of them homeless, loitering in the same block, hoping kind strangers will treat them to a pint. But before I can run or yell for help, I'm inside the car.

"You couldn't just call?" I ask Big Boy as he wipes ketchup from his mouth. I'm in the middle of the backseat, wedged between him and one of the teenage mentee gangbangers who pushed me in here.

"Just wanted to see how you were coming along," he says, "with the reverend and all."

I give him the short version, being sure to leave off the names, mentioning only Alderman. I'm hoping he doesn't insist on names. Big Boy and his minions could do me a lot more damage than a few days in jail for refusing to divulge a source.

"Alderman. Huh. So maybe this dude that they're about to put up a statue of on Monument Avenue, maybe he's behind some of this?"

I tell Big Boy that I don't know.

"I'm pretty sure, though, that McNish is innocent."

Big Boy nods his head.

"Thass good. You on the right track now."

"What do you mean, right track. Do you know something I ought to know?"

"When I think you ought to know something else, I'll make sure you know it. But what about Alderman? Any idea who carved his ass up?"

I confess ignorance. The conversation is making me a little uneasy, as is the fact that we're over in Big Boy's territory now, blocks from anything the gentrifiers are casting their eyes on as yet.

Big Boy scratches his gray, neatly trimmed beard and clears his throat.

"I want to thank you again for kind of looking out for Shorty," he says. "He says they're treating him right at that club. Says he could get full health insurance if he lasts a year, won't have to depend on Obamacare to save his ass."

I'm sure this is not all about Big Boy's undying gratitude. I wait for it.

"The thing is," he says, "if what you suspect about James Alderman is true, don't you think it's appropriate that somebody turn loose a mess of Old Testament justice on him?"

I allow that this could be, but the police aren't going to let go of this one ever. The outrage over one James Alderman being butchered outweighs the black community's outrage over the long-missing boys.

"Yeah," he says, "I hear that. You're in kind of a bind, Willie. You've gotta prove the man ain't no saint. I expect you'll feel some heat on your butt trying to write something about that."

You don't even know, I tell him.

Big Boy eventually, to my relief, has his driver turn around and head back south of the interstate. When they stop to let me off on the same block where I was grabbed, maybe thirty minutes ago, he has one piece of advice.

"McNish is a good man. He's been there for us for years. I don't for a minute believe he did anything to those kids. I hope you don't mind me getting a little personally involved here.

"That other guy, Alderman? I'd be happy as a pig in shit if you got the goods on him, since it seems like the police ain't exactly on top of it. But as to who killed the man, I'd appreciate it if you would just leave that one to the cops. Eye for an eye and all that. You get me?"

He puts one of his big, beefy paws on my right arm and squeezes to make his point. As I'm getting out, the kid who grabbed me looks me in the eye and puts his hand behind his back, like a guy with heat tucked in his waistband might do.

Message received.

WALKING BACK to the Prestwould, I ponder my next move. What I know about James Alderman sheds new light, more like a spotlight, on the case of the missing boys. It should at least make L.D. Jones and his crack staff question their infallible wisdom in locking up McNish.

But anything I write about Alderman will be done at my extreme peril. Nobody except maybe Big Boy Sunday and me seems to want to hear a discouraging word about the guy—not even the guy who's in the lockup, facing the possibility of life in prison or execution for a crime I'm sure he didn't commit. And what if Ray-Ray Soles was wrong? Just because he's still sure he's fingered the right guy twenty years ago doesn't mean maybe he didn't pick the wrong mug shot to begin with.

Painting one of our town's more saintly individuals as a possible monster is not only unhealthy to my career, but I could be wrong. It has happened. And, like doctors, I do subscribe to the "first, do no harm" rule.

Further roiling my troubled waters is Big Boy's "suggestion" that I not look too deeply into who killed Alderman. The conclusion is obvious, but I'd rather wait for the cops to figure this one out. If there's one man in this town I don't want thinking I'm out to get him, it's Big Boy Sunday.

Somehow I will make sure our readers know all or some of what I know. Figuring out how to make that happen and stay employed and alive is the trick.

PEGGY, ANDI, and little William are waiting for me when I come by at five. It's already dark, and it feels twenty degrees colder than it did this afternoon. Andi and I manage to wrestle the car seat into submission, and off we go.

We drive by the park where Artesian Cole's body was found. I take a quick detour, out of curiosity. We wrote in the paper this morning that a shrine of sorts had been erected there by the lake in his memory. Soon we find ourselves in a traffic jam. Others had the same idea, driving slowly past a live tree that's been adorned with ornaments and photographs. As we get closer, I see that the photos are blowups, encased in protective plastic, of the five kids we know who disappeared and, with the exception of Artesian, never resurfaced.

A gigantic star, almost as big as the tree, sits on a stand next to it. It's glowing red, reflected in the water. I can hear a generator running somewhere. On the star is a sign with one word, also in red: Justice.

Among the people standing in the cold and singing carols, I'm pretty sure I spot Laquinta Cole. I wonder how many mothers of the other boys who went missing are there.

I'm thinking that L.D. Jones needs to have a damn good alternative suspect before he releases Sam McNish. Those fifty people standing out here on a freezing December night aren't going to settle for anything less. There won't be any peace on earth if he lets the only viable suspect go.

"If it was my boy," I hear Peggy say in the darkness, "I'd be over at the courthouse, or the police station, or somewhere, every damn day until I got some answers."

It'll come to that, I assure my mother, if somebody doesn't tie up the loose ends soon.

The lights are dazzling, even if William does fall asleep halfway through our trek into this winter wonderland that must be making the electric company rich. The look on his face when we first got out of the car, though, was worth my freezing my butt off. One little toothless smile makes my night.

Of course, William has that same look of awe and delight when a dog comes up and licks his face.

CHAPTER SIXTEEN

Saturday

I've never had so much information with so little opportunity to publish it. Promises have been made, identities have been sworn to secrecy, jobs (mine, to be exact) hang in peril. So much can't be proved, yet every instinct I have tells me what I need to write is true.

It won't do much good to talk to Rita Dominick, for whom the best news stories are the ones that don't rile the power structure. A career in advertising does that to you.

There is one possible option. I know Wheelie likes to come in early on Saturdays and get some work done before staffers arrive and distract him by putting out the Sunday paper.

I get there at nine, well rested and wondering if Penny Lane suffered much from my absence last night.

As I had hoped, Mal Wheelwright is in his office.

"Got a minute?" I ask. He seems a bit pained but says yes. He probably knows that it isn't going to be anything like a minute, and that I'm not here to make his life any damn easier.

"It's about the Cole boy's murder. And James Alderman."

"Good God," Wheelie mutters. "Do you want to get us both fired?"

I lay it out as succinctly as I can:

- No evidence points to Sam McNish as the murderer beyond the fact that he was the last one known to see the boy alive.

- Stories about some creepy white guy hanging around poor neighborhoods have been out there so long that "Frosty" has become kind of an urban legend. And they go back so far that McNish could hardly be that guy.

- The late James Alderman, who helped as a mentor with the Children of God program, once was accused of trying to abduct a black kid who, as a present-day adult, freely admits that his now-dead mother got him to retract his accusation in exchange for someone paying off her mortgage. Another source with the police says L.D. Jones was there when it happened.

- And Alderman's rather gruesome slaying seems, because of the time frame if nothing else, to be linked to Artesian Cole's murder. A source I can't name is as much as telling me that.

"A lot of unnamed sources and maybes in there," Wheelie says. "Maybe you need to get some names."

I explain that naming names will not be possible. I further explain that we would be doing some good, honest journalism if we ran what we know and let people draw their own conclusions.

"She will fire us both, on the spot," Wheelie says.

I suggest that I can write something for tomorrow's paper that does not name James Alderman at all but raises considerable red flags about McNish's guilt.

"If we get our foot in the damn door," I tell Wheelie, "maybe we can kick the son of a bitch in later."

He sighs.

"Write it," he says. "I'll take a look at it. I can't promise we'll run it. Write it so it doesn't get us fired or sued, and I'll think about it."

And so I do. I call Sarah Goodnight, who comes in on what ought to be her day off. She's dressed the way you should dress on a Saturday when you're not even getting paid, but on her it looks good: the kind of jeans that a woman should only wear when she has no blemishes to hide and a white blouse on which she might have buttoned one more button at the top, but who's complaining?

Cindy has said to wait for her to call first regarding our future. Sitting there, with Sarah beside me as we do one of the most awkward things in journalism—cowrite a story—I get a whiff of her scent. If you've ever slept with a woman once and were really paying attention, you will remember that scent. A horndog never forgets. I am hoping Cindy calls soon.

What we finally send to Wheelie at one thirty has plenty to suggest McNish didn't do the deed. It mentions the lack of evidence. It mentions Frosty and all the permanently disappeared kids over the years. It regurgitates some quotes from some of their mothers, and Sarah manages to get some fresh reaction as well. It mentions the boy all those years ago who accused a pillar of the community of attempted abduction, without mentioning the boy's or the pillar's names. It mentions a check the boy's mother accepted when the boy recanted. It does all this without naming anyone except the mothers of the missing. Gunderson becomes "a source who was then a police officer." Ray-Ray Soles is "the boy who said he was accosted, now an adult living in Richmond." Some background from Big Boy Sunday we attribute to "a source in the black community familiar with the case." I hate using unnamed sources. It puts me in bed with writers who make shit up. But sometimes playing by the rules isn't enough.

Even Sarah doesn't know the identity of Soles, Gunderson, and Big Boy. I tell her the less she knows, the less likely she'll have to spend a night or two in jail for refusing to name sources.

Wheelie doesn't want to run it. When I take him down the story, graf by graf, and show him that we haven't actually libeled anyone, he insists that I tell him my sources. So I do, trusting that Wheelie is still enough of a newspaperman not to throw any of them under the bus. I actually threaten him with physical harm if he tells anyone, and especially our publisher.

"I don't think you're allowed to threaten the editor," Wheelie says.

I tell him that you can do anything once.

Finally, after I've taken out the juicy revelation that our present police chief was there twenty years ago when Ray-Ray Soles took back his accusation, he sighs and says he guesses we can run it. The much-awaited A1 blockbuster that blows the lid off the amazing rise of microbreweries and fruit-flavored beer in the greater Richmond area will have to wait until next Sunday.

Give Wheelie credit. He could have wimped out of this one by sending it to the publisher, who is up somewhere in Vermont skiing. He briefly considers it, then says, "Nah. Fuck it. She just said you couldn't write about James Alderman. Am I right?"

Right as rain, I assure him. We are both sure, though, that
her wrath will be upon us when she gets back in a couple of
days—before then if she can crawl her ass out of the hot tub
long enough to read our online edition.

I don't call the chief. I should give him a heads-up, but I
don't trust L.D., not after word of my suspicions about Alderman beat me back to the office last time we talked. He'll just
have to read it in the paper like everyone else. It won't be the
first time I've made him spit his cornflakes. Maybe he'll think
twice before he rats me out to the publisher again.

I do check in with Peachy Love. She can at least have a
running start on damage control before the shit hits the fan.
I extract a promise that the chief won't hear about it until the
paper hits his front doorstep. I tell her the part about L.D.
that we're not running.

"Jesus Christ," Peachy says. "He was there? Man, when I
put you onto Gunderson, I didn't know that."

I tell her not to worry, that nothing will splash up on her.
Gunderson doesn't know who pointed me to him.

"Well, I'm not looking forward to Monday. Hell, you
might even have caused me to get called in on Sunday. You
owe me more than flowers for this one, Willie."

I check my cell phone and see a familiar number on it. I
go down to the deserted end of our once-bustling newsroom.

"Willie," the much-anticipated voice on the other end
says, "can we talk?"

She called forty-five minutes ago. I have a bad habit of
accidentally muting my phone. That or the fact that I can't
hear shit when there's a lot of background noise caused me to
miss the call I've been waiting for since two days ago.

When I call Cindy back, it flips over into voice mail.

I explain, trying not to sound needy, that I somehow
missed her call and to please call me back as soon as possible.

To my great relief, she does, five long minutes later.

"OK," she says.

I wait.

"I'm a glutton for punishment. I love abuse."

"That sounds like good news, at least for me."

She sighs.

"I've always thought that it was a waste of time to try to change what can't be changed. And I've decided I am happier with you than without you, warts and all."

I start my tired-ass promise to be better. She stops me.

"I know you will try, Willie. I don't doubt that. But, you know, old dogs and new tricks. I'll hope for the best and brace myself for the worst."

I promise her that this old dog will do his best.

"I'll sit up and beg if you want."

I think I hear a chuckle, certainly a heartening sign.

"Make me proud," she says. "Make me proud to be seen with you."

I'm almost moved to tears. The knowledge that I have brought shame to someone I'd chew off my right arm to be with makes my chest hurt.

I can't think of much to say that won't sound like bullshit.

"I promise one thing," I say when I get the lump out of my throat. "I will make you happy."

"I believe that. If I didn't, we wouldn't be having this conversation."

"When can I see you?"

She says she is busy tonight.

I don't ask with what or whom she is busy. I'm not holding a hot hand right now. No need in pushing it.

"Tomorrow night?"

She says that would be fine. As we hang up, I tell her I love her. Again, really pushing my luck.

"You, too," she says.

It's more than I deserve.

A SHOOTING in the East End becomes a fatality when one of the gun-toting teenagers dies at the scene. I'm standing there, looking at a white sheet covering a wasted life and wondering why we can't at least have a Christmas truce. The cops are already bundling the other shooter into a van. He's headed for a life that probably won't be a big step above a dirt nap.

Out of the corner of my eye, I see a rather large black woman approaching me.

"When are you all going to write something about that man been killin' our babies?" she says, loudly. I don't think this woman says anything softly. It is a phenomenon I see often in our poorer neighborhoods. Speaking softly, the powerless understand, does not get people's attention.

Others wander over, some echoing the woman's frustration, others just looking for more entertainment on this cold, hopeless night. They know me here, since my ass is on their streets far too often. To them, I'm just part of the big white establishment. I'm The Man. I'm not black enough to be black in the East End. I see a couple of cops watching from a safe distance, enjoying my discomfort.

Just then, a woman breaks through the crowd. Laquinta Cole stands in front of me and faces them.

"Leave him alone," she says. "He's doing the best he can."

She commands enough respect that she doesn't have to shout it. She's accorded deference. Around here, she's like those Gold Star Mothers who lost a child in a war. Hell, this is a war.

There is more grumbling, but then a fight breaks out back in the crowd and my fifteen seconds of fame are thankfully over. Farther back, watching from a safe distance, I see Big Boy Sunday, surrounded by kids about the age of the one who just died, seeking to curry his favor. I wonder if Laquinta came here with him.

I thank her for having my back and promise her that we are far from done with getting to the truth.

She looks at me and shakes her head.

"Truth is hard to come by around here," she says. "Truth, justice, we don't get too much of that."

She turns to walk away but then turns back around and gives me a better understanding of why she stood up for me.

"But we do appreciate what you did for Shorty," she says.

I'm almost to my beat-up Honda when my cell phone rings. This time, I hear it. It's almost eleven thirty. Usually, that's the office wondering whether I'm going to file or not. This one won't get more than a couple of grafs on B2, it being so late and our deadlines getting earlier every time we get some new technology. Plus, it is the East End.

If it isn't the office, it's usually bad news.

This time, it's neither.

I can't hear the other party that well, so I get in the car and shut the door. Finally I recognize the voice.

"I need to tell you something," Sam McNish says.

I ask him how he's managed to call me from the lockup this late at night.

"One of the guards," he says. "He had a son that went to Children of God. I guess he thinks I helped more than hurt. At least he doesn't think I'm guilty."

So the guard, no doubt breaking a few rules, loaned McNish his cell phone. I'm waiting, letting him do the talking. Whatever he wants to tell me is worth my patience. People don't call you from the jail at damn near midnight to chew the fat.

"It's about James Alderman."

He admits he was angry yesterday. The idea of his mentor and longtime friend being involved in the unthinkably heinous was not something he was willing to even contemplate.

"But then I started thinking," he says. "And something came to me. I'm sorry to call you so late, but it just occurred to me. And I felt as if I had to tell you."

"What occurred to you?"

"That you might be right."

CHAPTER SEVENTEEN

Sunday

What Sam McNish told me last night made me miss my deadline, although we did get the latest homicide in on the replate. Sally Velez was pissed, but it was worth it.

At least, sitting here this morning a couple of houses down from James Alderman's place on Seminary, I think it was.

What McNish remembered was a casual remark, one of those things that don't mean much to you at the time but hit you like a runaway truck later.

"If what I fear is true," McNish said, "it will shake my faith in everything I've done. It will be as if I've spent my whole life on the wrong path."

I'm guessing that he figured having his faith shaken was at least a pinch less devastating than standing trial for a murder or five. Or maybe he just wants justice.

"Why didn't you tell the cops about this?"

"I don't think they'd believe me. They might think I was making it up, that I'd done it myself, or that I was his accomplice. Plus, it just came to me."

Like a vision, I wanted to say, but making fun of the man's religion right then would not have been smart or kind.

What McNish remembered was this:

Several years ago—he said he thought it was at least five—he was having lunch with Alderman in the house I'm just about to break into.

They were having a philosophical conversation, which seems to me like a perfect way to spoil a good meal, but to each his own.

"We were talking about good and evil, about whether some people are born evil, whether there are souls that belong to the devil before they're even born."

Sitting there drinking coffee afterward, McNish said his spiritual guide told him he needed to share something with him that he had never shared with another human being.

"It made me uneasy. He had this strange look to him, like I'd never seen before. We'd killed a bottle of wine and half another one with lunch, and maybe it made him more open. I don't know.

"He told me to follow him. He walked over to this china hutch in the corner of his dining room, and he unlocked it with a key he had in his pocket. He knelt and he lifted up this little gravy boat on the bottom shelf. Underneath it, he slid a little block of wood forward, and hidden under it was another key."

He told McNish that, in the event of his death, he should retrieve that key. McNish asked him what the key was for. He said Alderman just smiled and told him that it could answer any lingering questions he might have about the nature of good and evil.

"He said, 'I hope, Samuel'—that's what he called me—'that you won't be too disappointed in what you find.'"

"And then he put the key back and slid the block of wood over the top of it and laid the gravy boat back on top."

When McNish asked him to be more specific, he said Alderman told him that a "smart lad" like him should be able to figure it out eventually.

"But he said something, as I was leaving. He gave me this little smile and said that, if you wanted to find evil, it was traditional to look downward."

McNish said they never discussed it again.

"I just forgot about it. It didn't make much sense at the time. And then he never mentioned it afterward, and I didn't think about it again, not even after I heard he was murdered. Until yesterday."

I told McNish that this sounded like pretty thin gruel, not exactly what you would hang your hat on if you were the chief of police.

"Well, maybe that's why I called you," he said. "You go on hunches sometimes, don't you? Well, I don't usually, but I'm feeling a pretty good one right now."

I told McNish I would see what I could do, and he hung up.

EVEN WITHOUT my felonious plans for this Sabbath morning, it's been an eventful day so far.

Turns out that Rita Dominick was able to rouse herself from the joys of skiing in Vermont to check our website this morning . . . about five, apparently. My story on the unnamed James Alderman and the murder of Artesian Cole caught her eye, and not in a good way.

By the time she got through burning Wheelie's ears and he called me, it was almost six, not my favorite time of any day.

"She wants you to call her," Wheelie said. I reminded him that we agreed that this story should run.

"Yeah," he said, "but maybe we should have talked to the publisher first."

I could see a bus coming. I'm standing on the curb, and Wheelie's behind me.

"But you told her you OK'd it, right?"

A slight pause.

"Sure."

Shit.

I didn't bother to tell Wheelie what a no-guts move he'd made, just reminded him that I'm going to need backup. No point in burning bridges. If I don't get fired, Wheelie's still my newsroom boss.

"I'm with you, Willie," he said and gave me her phone number.

Wheelie, I understand, is with me until he isn't.

Since our publisher obviously was already wide awake and loaded for bear, there was no sense in delaying my call.

"What were you thinking?" is the way she greeted her star reporter.

I answered a question with a question.

"Did you see James Alderman's name anywhere in that story?"

"I didn't have to. Half the town probably knows who we're talking about by now."

I asked her how that could be.

She dodged my question.

"I told you not to write anything about Alderman, didn't I? Didn't I tell you that?"

I was getting a little tired of being lectured like a second-grader before the damn sun had even come up. I expressed this sentiment to Ms. Dominick and further drove home the point, which should be obvious to anyone but an idiot, that we have in no way identified James Alderman as a potential murderer and child molester.

"You can't talk to me like that!"

I assured her that I can and have. I further explained that there likely will be more information coming about Alderman. Furthermore, I told her, I had a feeling what I dig up will be so hot she will either have to sign off on it or read about it in the *Washington Post* while our readers wonder just how far we have managed to jam our heads up our own asses.

Finally she said the magic words.

"You're fired. When I get back, I'll make it official."

And she hung up.

Having no desire to talk to her anymore, I didn't call back. Instead I called Wheelie and told him what had transpired.

"One thing, though, that you can do for me," I told him.

"What?"

"Pretend I'm not fired, at least until she gets back. After all, she said she'd make it official then."

"But what if she tells me, flat out, to have you escorted out of the building?"

"Avoid her phone calls, Wheelie. You've got some vacation coming. Get out of town until Wednesday, and I guarantee you it'll be worth your while."

I expressed some disappointment that our publisher has reached new depths in suppressing the news.

There's a pause, then Wheelie said, "There's something you need to know, Willie. But it didn't come from me."

Wait for it.

"There's a group interested in buying the paper."

No surprise there. We've had people sniffing around here for the last year and a half, but nothing's come of it so far.

"These guys are pretty serious, but here's the capper, and you have to keep it under your hat."

I took the vow of silence.

"One of the partners in this holding company is Lee Alderman. James Alderman's brother."

The veil was lifted. Some money-grubbing holding company wants to buy us, and I'm in the process of taking a very large crap on the brother of one of the partners.

"I wish somebody had told me," I said.

"Would it have made any difference?"

Probably not, but at least I'd have had more of a storm warning.

At any rate, Wheelie promised to make himself scarce for a couple of days, turn off the cell phone and hide. I'm betting that Dominick won't get someone below Wheelie to do the deed and will wait until she gets home. She probably would prefer dropping the blade herself anyhow.

So I have miles to go if I want to keep this Christmas even marginally merry for me and my loved ones. I have to pin the tail on the donkey before my publisher gets back. Even that might not be enough, but you have to try.

Which is why I'm sitting here now as the last remnants of heat seep out of my Honda. I have to act now or make myself more suspicious than I, and my ancient chariot, already are in this well-tended neighborhood.

Fortunately I'm in a community of churchgoers. It being the Sunday morning before Christmas, the place seems pretty dead.

I'm not bursting with good ideas. What McNish said, though, does pique my interest. I do have an inspiration about what to do when I get inside Chez Alderman, assuming I don't get caught for breaking and entering. The fact that the accused seems so sure about his hunch the day after so vigorously defending Alderman gives me some comfort that this is not a fool's errand.

A lot of these blocks have alleyways bisecting them, leading to garages. It's a relatively easy way for someone to slip into someone else's house without being seen from the street. Alderman's place, in particular, has a nice stand of boxwoods around the back fence that must be a burglar's delight.

I walk down the alleyway until I come to the back of Alderman's house. There is a gate leading into a yard that's covered with oak and sycamore leaves. I manage to flip open the latch with nothing more than a stick. Until recently, people along Seminary felt pretty safe, I'm guessing.

Coming up on the back porch elevates me enough to expose me to anyone looking directly across from the house that backs up to the alley on the other side, but I don't see any cars in the driveway. I press on.

There is crime tape around the back door, but when I try the handle, it turns. For all I know, this is the way the killer entered last week and nobody ever bothered to lock it again.

Inside, the place smells musty, like the old man's house it was. There's another smell underneath that, something I can't put my finger on but suspect involves the prelude to a violent death.

With the blinds drawn, it's almost too dark to see. I take a chance and turn on a light. In the living room, there's a rug that looks more expensive than my car, but the stain that has soaked a good two square feet of it is probably going to devalue it somewhat. This is where James Alderman spent his last moments, and I don't think they were happy ones.

Something else catches my eye, lying on the floor next to the kitchen trash can. I pick it up and put it in my pocket.

It doesn't take me long to find the china hutch, a magnificent piece of furniture made out of some kind of dark wood.

Like the boxwoods outside, it smells of money and elegance to a guy from Oregon Hill, where the furniture was mostly pine or plastic and shrubbery was whatever would grow.

Since I obviously don't have access to James Alderman's key ring, I have to do a little B&E. Since I've already broken into his house, cracking a pane in the hutch probably won't add much to my damn sentence.

So I reach inside, cutting myself slightly on the broken glass, and open it. The gravy boat is right where McNish said it would be, on the bottom shelf. And, as advertised, there's a piece of wood underneath that slides out and exposes what looks like a very old key.

But what's it for? And why did Alderman tell McNish about it? And what the hell am I supposed to do with it?

I have a general idea. The house has a basement, like most of the places along here. The door, down at the end of a long hallway, is open. I am glad that there is a light switch at the top of the stairs. This place is giving me the damn creeps. It's starting to remind me of the haunted house we kids used to go to on Halloween. The stairs creak, and I wonder when the unseen hand is going to grab me and make me crap myself.

My eyes gradually adjust to the dim light at the bottom. I look around but don't see anything that you wouldn't see in most basements—discarded furniture, suitcases, all kinds of memorabilia, the kind of stuff the survivors wind up giving to the Salvation Army just to haul it away.

The key in my left hand is looking pretty useless. There was no keyhole to the door leading down here. Whatever Alderman meant about looking down doesn't seem to apply here.

But then I spot something, peeking out maybe a foot over the top of a large dresser that sits behind several boxes of God-knows-what. I look around and realize that the basement isn't nearly as large as the entire first floor area above it. What I see is the top of a door.

It takes me ten minutes to move the boxes out of the way and then wrestle the dresser, which apparently is loaded with ball bearings, out of the way.

Behind it is the door. It has a keyhole.

It's locked, of course. When I try the key, it doesn't work at first either. I jiggle it this way and that and am about to give up when, finally, I hold my mouth just right and the key turns. And the door opens.

It is dark and dank. It smells of wet clay, because there's only a dirt floor back here. I realize that I should have brought a flashlight, since I can't see shit, no matter how long I stand there. So I go back upstairs and eventually find one. Its weak-ass light makes me fear that its batteries haven't been changed lately.

But it'll have to do.

Looking around the finished part of the basement, I see a shovel. It seems odd that it would be here, rather than, say, in a tool shed. Out of some instinct, I take it with me into the dark. Hell, if nothing else, maybe I can use it to beat back the rats. This place is not growing on me.

I go forward, a step at a time, the shovel in one hand and the flashlight in the other. I have only about a foot of head-room. There doesn't seem to be much down here except dirt.

But then I trip. I'm on my hands and knees, with goose bumps all over, tasting Virginia clay. I find the flashlight and shine it on what tripped me. Just more dirt, except it's raised a few inches. Just enough to trip someone who's stumbling around in the dark.

I shine the light farther down, toward the back wall. There are at least half a dozen of those bumps, in a neat little row.

The heat pump comes on, the bump and roar making me jump high enough to hit my head on a beam. I take deep breaths until I can't hear my heart thumping anymore.

I look down at my hand and realize I am holding the shovel. It's as if I knew what I was here for.

I start to dig.

The shovel hits nothing but thick, stubborn earth for the first fifteen minutes or so. Then I hit something that clanks against the metal. I don't really want to see what I've dug up, but that's what I'm down here for. The flashlight batteries seem to be fading, but when I shine the weak yellow light down into the small pit I've dug, I see something off-white. I get as low as I can, with one leg in the pit and the other kneeling at ground level, and I brush away the dirt with my free hand.

There's no denying what I'm touching anymore. The skull belonged to a human being.

A rustling in the near distance might be rats or my imagination. Whichever, I'm out of that hole in about two seconds. I don't spend more than a minute getting out of the late James Alderman's house. This time, I don't really give a damn who sees me.

I'm back home at the Prestwould by twelve thirty or so, just as our building's churchgoers are returning home for Sunday dinner or getting ready to head back out for brunch. A flock of them are standing in front of the building chatting when I walk up.

Feldman, who's Jewish but just naturally shows up anywhere there might be gossip, remarks that I look like I've had a hard morning.

I tell him that he really doesn't want to know.

Custalow is watching the NFL pregame show. He is getting ready to dig into a delivery pizza. He is kind enough to offer me a slice and not ask me why I look like I've been digging ditches. He says I got a call from someone who said I'd know who it was and left a number. I recognize the publisher's cell phone from earlier.

"She was pretty rude," Custalow says.

Fuck her, I explain.

If Rita Dominick wants to chew on my ass a little more, she's going to have to come back here and do it in person.

CHAPTER EIGHTEEN

Monday

Yesterday might have been, on paper, the shortest day of the year. From my perspective, it was just a bit long.

After I got cleaned up, I called Cindy to tell her that I could be late for our much-anticipated (by me, at least) makeup date this evening. The silence that followed compelled me to swear her to secrecy and tell her what exactly might be occupying me for the next few hours.

"Jesus, Willie," she said. "You really do know how to mess up Christmas."

After that, it seemed only decent that I call L.D. Jones and give him the happy news. I also informed him that our online audience would be reading about it in a couple of hours. "Human remains found at home of murdered theologian" might even get the restless and horny to turn away from their favorite porn sites for a while.

"You can't write that shit," L.D. said. He was actually, from the sound of it, sputtering. "You can't tell people there were human remains there. How can you be sure, goddammit?"

I admonished him not to take the Lord's name in vain, and I told him that I would stake what paltry reputation I have on the fact that it was indeed a human skull I found about two feet below the dirt floor in James Alderman's basement.

You can't run stuff like that in the paper, where we still insist on pesky stuff like proven facts. Our website, though, seems to have a slightly lower standard. As much as I bitch about giving the news away online, it is a great place to tell what you know but can't prove.

I'd never post this, I told the chief, if I wasn't absolutely, positively sure.

He asked me how I got in. I told him I let myself in.

"I'm going to arrest your ass," he said. "Breaking and entering. Adulterating a crime scene."

"Adulterating?"

"Even if what you saw was bones, how can you link that to those missing kids?"

I pointed out that my report would say nothing that would link the skull I found to any of the boys whose disappearances surfaced in the wake of Artesian Cole's murder.

"Well, people will draw that conclusion."

Yeah, I thought. The ones with half a brain will.

"You shouldn't have been there," L.D. says. "You should have called the police if you suspected something."

I reminded him that I had expressed my concerns already, and all it got me was a bitching out by my publisher after some unknown person tipped her off that I was snooping around Alderman.

He sighs.

"Alderman. Goddamn."

"Do you want to know where to dig?"

He was silent. Finally, he said yes, much in the manner that I imagine Socrates accepted his hemlock.

After I told him what he needed to know, he hung up without saying good-bye.

It went pretty fast after that.

I had convinced our web masters that we had to put this up right then, and put it up where it would be the first thing freeloaders saw when they went to our site. It didn't take long to write what I'd discovered so far. One body discovered, with indications of other graves alongside it. I figured, correctly, that the TV stations would be all over it, even though the only place housing fewer journalists on a Sunday afternoon than a daily newspaper is a TV studio. Fine with me. When the good-hair people poach a story like this, with no substantiation behind it other than one newspaper reporter's eyeballs, they always attribute the source, to cover their butts in case we're wrong.

By the time I got back over to Seminary, the place was a crime scene on steroids. Half the force seemed to be there. I could only get as far as the curb before I was stopped. It didn't seem wise to explain that I was the guy who broke in earlier and found the remains. As soon as L.D. gets far enough ahead of the news to think about it, he'll be looking to arrest me anyhow.

All four local stations were already there. Bleary-eyed cameramen and "personalities" who hadn't had time to mousse their hair were scurrying about like deranged squirrels, trying to find somebody who knew something and breathlessly telling their listeners what I'd told them on our website. They know me, and I was hounded more than the cops. I told one kid reporter that they thought they'd found Jimmy Hoffa. It was obvious the kid didn't know who the hell Jimmy Hoffa was. I got to say "no comment" a lot, as well as my favorite: "You can read about it in the paper tomorrow."

Gillespie was avoiding me, apparently not ready to repay me for all those donuts with some news I could use. The other cops, even if they didn't dislike me personally, knew the chief would skin them if they were seen in my company.

But I saw four people from the coroner's office come and go, and guys with hazmat suits were in and out for the next two hours, apparently afraid of catching cooties from the long-since dead.

My luck turned, though, when I saw Peachy Love. Even the media relations folks were scrambled for this one, which was going to take a lot of spinning, especially if it became known that L.D. Jones was there the day James Alderman was exonerated for cash two decades ago.

I didn't try to get close to Peachy, or even acknowledge that we knew each other. She's one source I definitely do not want to burn. I have, though, learned how to text. I let Peachy know I'd be calling her later. No response. I was crossing my fingers that she would answer though.

The chief did have to give a press conference, since every news outlet in town was following him around. He said that there was evidence of what appeared to be human remains inside, being sure to add that the earlier web report was "reckless and inaccurate," and that there would be more information as the investigation progressed.

Asked why the bodies weren't found during the fine-tooth-comb search the police did earlier, he said there was a hidden room. It sounded pretty lame, and L.D. looked like he needed either bourbon or Pepto Bismol.

They asked him if the bodies had any connection to Artesian Cole's death or the other boys from the past who went missing. He had no comment.

It was dark by the time the crime scene started getting depopulated. I had already told Sally Velez what we had, in case she wasn't monitoring the website.

Sally knew we were supposed to handle Alderman with kid gloves. With the cops acknowledging that human remains were found, though, all bets were off.

"I can't seem to find Wheelie," she said, "but we're going to go with it. Hell, it's been on every local station already."

Good old Wheelie. Stay low awhile longer, Boss.

I'd been feeding the web when I had time.

Back at the office, I called Peachy. She answered, and she didn't hang up when I told her who it was.

She told me enough. They found at least six sets of human remains, pretty much intact. They appeared to be those of juvenile males, and they'd been buried for some years. She sounded pretty shook up. I promised her, as always, that waterboarding couldn't make me reveal my source.

What Peachy told me was enough to meet the newspaper's (well, at least my) standards. I told Sally what I knew, without telling her who gave it to me. She didn't have to ask. I also told her about my tenuous employment situation. If Rita Dominick didn't like what would be leading today's paper, I added, maybe she could hire me again just so she could have the thrill of firing me twice.

"Well," Sally said, "I just hope she doesn't come after me too. I've still got some good years left, unlike you. I don't want to spend them freelance editing."

"You don't know anything," I told her. "I didn't tell you I was technically fired, and Wheelie sure as hell didn't."

"I don't guess you know where he is."

"Not a clue."

Sarah came in to help out. She got in touch with four of the mothers of the missing boys, whose response was what you would expect from someone who has maybe carried a little flicker of hope over the years and has seen it quite possibly snuffed out, someone who has expected the worst and now has to live with it.

By the time I'd filed the story, it was past eight thirty. As always, the really bad days are the best ones to be a reporter, and the time flew by.

When I'd been fairly well assured that the copy desk wasn't going to do violence to the story, I left.

It took fifteen minutes to get to Cindy's house. I was somewhat relieved to see that lights were on inside, which gave me hope that she hadn't gone out on the town with parties unknown. It didn't eliminate the possibility that she was spending a cozy evening at home with someone else. Who could blame her?

But when she answered, in the kind of housecoat no woman would wear while entertaining overnight guests of the male persuasion, I figured I still had a chance.

"Some date you turned out to be," she said, but she smiled a little.

Standing in the doorway, I gave her the sneak preview of tomorrow's Willie Black special. She said she'd been following it on our online site, which I'd updated four times during the afternoon and evening.

"You're not a subscriber anymore?"

"Who under sixty is?"

She saw the hurt in my eyes and said she still gets the "special" weekend package we more or less give away.

I asked her if she was going to ask me in.

"What for?" she said. "Don't you have a home?"

I thought I'd take a chance.

"It's kind of cold sleeping by yourself on a night like this."

She shook her head, said my name three times, and wondered what she was going to do with me.

I had a suggestion.

"Well," she said, opening the door wider, "come on in. I'm freezing my butt off. You're letting all the heat out."

Maybe, I suggested, we could both use a little warmth.

I RAN out and got a paper this morning from the market a couple of blocks from Cindy's place.

"Remains found in Alderman's basement," screamed the headline. "As many as six bodies; possible tie to Cole slaying," said the subhead. We can't say Artesian Cole's death is related to those bodies, but it isn't too hard to connect the dots:

- Artesian's body turns up.

- It develops that at least four other kids fitting his general description have gone missing over two decades and were never found.

- Eight days later, James Alderman is butchered.

- Alderman was connected with the Children of God program, where he tutored, among others, Artesian Cole.

- Eight days after that, half a dozen boys' remains are found buried in Alderman's basement.

I wonder if my adoring publisher is already on her way back. But then I check the weather and see that it's snowing in the Northeast and flights are being scrubbed left and right out of New York. Truly a Christmas miracle. I have two missed calls from Ms. Dominick on my cell. I'll get around to those in a day or three.

I have a couple of cups of coffee with Cindy and wonder out loud if she will still have me when I'm on welfare.

"They're hiring at Walmart," she says. "Look, Willie, if I haven't ditched you yet, after all the ways you've fucked up, a little thing like unemployment probably isn't going to matter. We can always live with your mother. Oregon Hill will always take us back."

An involuntary shudder escapes me.

"Just kidding," Cindy says.

There are some calls, though, that need answering.

Kate wants me to know that there's a pretty good chance Sam McNish will be released on sensibly priced bail today. Marcus has already been working on it, apparently. I tell her that I want to be there when he gets out. What I really want is to be there to whisk him into Marcus's car for a nice, leisurely drive around town before we take him home, with the TV guys in hot pursuit.

"I don't think an exclusive is out of the question here," I tell Kate.

She agrees.

"You broke in?" she says. "That's a little extreme, even by your standards. Hell, Willie, you might be needing Marcus yourself pretty soon."

Could be, I agree, but it's going to look like a terminal case of poor sportsmanship if L.D. locks me up now, after I've done his spadework for him, using a literal spade.

"Well, I just hope you'll still be able to pay the rent after all this shakes down."

Anyone who thinks my status as ex-husband will buy me a grace period with Kate Ellis doesn't know Kate Ellis.

The other call is from Big Boy Sunday. I appreciate the fact that he is using his cell this time instead of abducting me.

"Looks like you did good, Willie," Big Boy says. "I hear they'll be springing that white boy today."

I start to ask him how he has that information, but I probably don't want to know.

I tell him that we still don't have a bead on who murdered James Alderman, and the cops can't say with complete certainty that those bodies have anything to do with his girlfriend's late son.

"Well, you know and I know what's what," he says. "Even the damn cops will be able to piece it all together now."

"Except maybe about Alderman. I mean, was he suddenly so wracked with guilt that he cut his own thumbs, dick, and balls off and stabbed and shot himself a few times for good measure? Seems a little extreme."

It's as good a time as any to tell Big Boy that we need to talk.

"What we need to talk about?"

"Something I found at Alderman's house. Something that concerns you."

"Ain't nothing at that place that concerns me, Willie."

"Still, you're going to want to hear this. Trust me."

He seems to be chewing on something.

Finally he says he can meet me tomorrow. He gives me an address in a part of town I don't particularly want to frequent without a bodyguard.

"No. This one has to be on my turf."

I tell him to meet me at the Prestwould at two o'clock.

"The Prestwould. Got damn! They won't even let me in that place. Probably call the police when they see me standing at the door."

I assure him that this will not be the case.

"There's a big lobby there. Nice and open. And one more thing: I'd appreciate it if you'd leave the help in the car. Your disciples make me a little nervous."

He laughs.

"They supposed to make you nervous, Willie. Hell, they make me nervous sometimes. But what makes you think you can give me marching orders these days?"

I mention what I found. I also mention that I've mailed a certain piece of information to two people I trust, two people who won't open that mail unless I disappear.

He grunts and hangs up.

THEY RELEASE Sam McNish on one hundred thousand bond at one thirty. Marcus Green posts it. He, Kate, and I usher McNish to Marcus's car, past the cameramen and TV reporters. One of them actually hangs on to the door and almost gets dragged along as we pull away. I ask Marcus if it would be possible to stop and back over a couple of the more ambitious ones.

There are a few protesters outside the jail. But anybody who can read pretty much knows they got the wrong man. None of them are exercised enough to join the news media in chasing Marcus down a city street. L.D. Jones chose to give this particular photo opportunity a miss.

I'm sitting in the backseat, beside McNish. He appears to be somewhat stunned.

"You were your own salvation," I remind him. He looks confused.

"The tip. About Alderman's basement."

"Oh. Yeah. I just can't believe . . . I couldn't see what was right in front of me. I could have stopped him. I could have saved Artesian."

I advise him to quit beating himself up. Nobody in this whole city had a clue what James Alderman was really like.

"Yeah," McNish says, "but I thought I knew him better than anyone else."

I tell him that I want to interview him, and that I'd like to do it today, before some other newshound finally tracks him down.

He turns to me.

"I owe you that. But can you give me a day? I just need to clear my head. I know you're not religious, Willie, but I need to pray. I need to know where God wants me to go next."

I ask him how and where he hopes to do that without interruption. There's bound to be a host of microphones and cameras waiting for him back at Grace of God. Somebody probably will be staking out the Prestwould and Marcus's law offices.

He shrugs.

I have an idea. Not necessarily a good idea, but something.

"How about Oregon Hill? My mother's place isn't on anybody's radar."

We drive around behind Peggy's, through the alley, and take him in through the back door, away from the eyes of her prying neighbors.

I explain it all to Peggy, who is only mildly stoned. I emphasize the fact that McNish needs some quiet time.

"Is it OK if I feed him?"

"Yeah, that'd be good. But you might not want to offer him a joint."

"He probably could use one."

What the hell. It certainly wouldn't be the first dope McNish smoked.

He promises to talk to me tomorrow at noon.

Marcus drops me off at the Prestwould. It is hard to believe that my workday is just starting. But there's plenty to write about, even without Sam McNish's interview.

I ask Marcus, as I'm getting out, how he plans to make a buck off this, since the profit motive is what mostly drives him.

"I mean, you probably don't get to try him in front of a jury. I don't think he's going to need your services anymore."

"Not unless he'd like to slap the police department with a big-ass civil suit. Nah, I don't think he'll do that. It wouldn't be charitable. Just look at it as my Christmas gift. Just call me ol' Santa Claus. I probably won't even bill him much for my services so far."

"Whatever you bill him," I tell Marcus, "you ought to give me half."

He laughs.

"Willie," he says, "I wouldn't insult you by offering you money when I know you're just doing what any good honest journalist would do."

Hell, Marcus will get enough free publicity out of this to make it worth his while.

Kate gets out of the car and gives me a hug as I head upstairs to change clothes and go to work.

"Thank you," she says. "And don't forget the rent's due on the first."

Not much chance of that. I wonder how long it'll take Rita Dominick to get from Vermont to Richmond.

If the meeting with Big Boy Sunday goes as expected, I might be able to give L.D. Jones a Christmas present he won't forget.

CHAPTER NINETEEN

Tuesday

McNish's release is, of course, front-page stuff, but every-body with a TV knew about that before supper yesterday. The trick was to give them something fresh in this morning's paper. I think we did that.

Sarah was able to get an exclusive interview with Laquinta Cole. I would be too modest if I didn't mention that I called Laquinta on my cell phone and asked her if the newspaper reporter who was coming over could talk to her without those pesky TV reporters around. I don't know if Artesian's mother has any warm feelings for me. I can imagine she is balled up enough in her own grief right now without having to worry about the needs of a damn reporter. But she is grateful that I helped Shorty get a job. I'm starting to regret her brother's failure to shoot our publisher, although it would not have been a good career move on his part.

And I do have a few snippets from Sam McNish, gleaned from our ride yesterday. The story coyly notes that Mr. McNish is in an undisclosed location, savoring his freedom.

It will take awhile to figure out who all those forever-lost kids were whose bodies were dug up in James Alderman's basement. There are actually two more bodies than there are grieving mothers. It speaks volumes that we have kids in this city who disappear and have nobody interested enough to mention it. It isn't something the Chamber of Commerce and tourism folks are likely to be trumpeting.

I DON'T think Rita Dominick is back in town yet. I say this because when I enter the building at nine thirty, nobody seizes my ID card. And L.D. probably is ass deep in alligators and hasn't had time yet to have me arrested as a cat burglar. So, still working and still free.

I make a few calls. Sarah is one of the few employees in the newsroom at this hour. Everyone's trying to use those vacation hours before they turn into pumpkins on January 1. She says she's headed out to talk to some of the mothers. She's also gotten a tip on who one of the other boys, as yet unnamed, might have been.

"So what else do you have up your sleeve?" she asks me. "Are you going to tell our readers tomorrow who killed James Alderman?"

I tell her it all depends.

"I was kidding. Really? You might have something on that?"

"Like I said, it depends. First, though, I've got to do an interview with the Reverend McNish."

I haven't bothered to tell Sarah that I have him stashed away. She looks a little hurt. Not the first time a woman has felt shut out by my tendency to keep my cards close.

I apologize to her and assure her that I never doubted she could keep a secret.

"I was just so busy yesterday. I'm sorry. I should have let you know."

"Well, yeah. It would have saved me some work. I've been trying to find him myself."

I ask her if she'd like to come along to Peggy's for the interview.

"No. I don't think so. I have to talk to a couple of the mothers. But I can't tell you which ones."

Touché.

Peggy fixed a late breakfast for McNish and Awesome Dude, and the two men are having an interesting theological chat when I get there. Awesome seems to be under the impression that reindeer were somehow part of the original nativity scene. McNish is gently correcting him.

"Willie," Awesome says, "this dude really knows his Scripture and shit."

McNish and I go back into the bedroom where Andi and my grandson sleep. It's the same one where I grew up, and the place still smells the same. The window I cracked trying to chip golf shots into a trash can is still there, unfixed. I'm willing to bet you could find some of my old baseball cards in the bottom drawer of the dresser. Peggy isn't so much sentimental as indifferent when it comes to changing things.

I ask McNish what hope he has for preserving Grace of God.

"Well," he says, "I do own the building. To my knowledge, I haven't done anything to get it condemned, although I'm told my neighbors have done a pretty good job of trashing the place."

The way he says "neighbors" is about as close to a show of venom as I've seen from Sam McNish. I ask him if he's bitter.

"Bitter? No. Not really. They want a nice neighborhood, and Grace of God scared them, especially the kids' program.

I've got no complaints, and I welcome them all to come worship with us.

"I just wish people could see that we're all in this together. Kids who get thrown to the wolves on the other side of town are our problem too. Even if your heart doesn't get it, your head ought to."

He says he understands why Stella Barnes might have thought he was a suspect in Artesian Cole's murder. I note that he is more understanding than I am.

He smiles and shakes his head.

"I could have been more kind to her."

He already has plans for getting things up and running again in the New Year. He said he contacted some of the aides and mentors yesterday after I dropped him off. Some of them are interested in coming back. Some aren't.

"Worst scenario? We move to another neighborhood and start over. But the kids and their parents? They're ready right now."

He reaches into this weather-beaten satchel and pulls out some letters. There are five of them, all written by boys who were in the Children of God program. I read enough of them to know Sam McNish hasn't lost his flock. Even before the facts more or less exonerated him, those kids had.

"And I have a whole stack that our worshippers sent me," he says. He pulls out a pile of letters three times as big as the one from the kids.

I ask him about James Alderman. He's obviously given his late mentor a lot of thought. He seems as confused as everyone else. He can't quite get his mind around the idea that there might be pure evil in the world. He seems so naive I want to put him in bubble wrap.

"I have always thought evil grew like cancer. Neglect or cruelty or mental illness or hardship of some kind embedded itself. And I thought it was treatable, curable."

He shakes his head.

"This, though, this is something else. I've heard about monsters like that Bundy guy who were evil for no apparent reason, but even then I thought there must be something that could explain it. Now, I'm not so sure."

I get the impression Sam McNish is a man to whom uncertainty is a new phenomenon, one that he's going to have to wrestle with.

We talk for forty-five minutes. Then he turns the gun on me.

"What about you, Willie? What do you believe in?"

Usually this is where I remind my subject that I'm there to ask questions, not answer them. This time, I feel the need to say something.

I tell him I believe in social justice, the Golden Rule, cold Millers, and forgiving women, in no particular order.

"And God?"

I tell him I'm not smart enough to know that one.

"Smart doesn't have a lot to do with it," he says. "But let me ask you something: If you're not sure, wouldn't it be a good idea to err on the side of caution?"

It isn't something I think about much, maybe because it leads to some uncomfortable answers.

"What I do know," I tell McNish, "is that I doubt a god who only gets my business because I'm afraid of hell and damnation would look all that kindly on a sinner like me who was just playing the odds. And a god that only wanted me to crawl in terror wouldn't be a god I'd want to be associated with."

"It doesn't have to be like that," McNish says. "If your love is unrequited, you don't act out of, as you say, 'terror.'"

Maybe that's the problem. Maybe I'm not the unrequited love type. Maybe, despite being married three times, I'm afraid of that kind of commitment.

At any rate, I promise Sam McNish that I will make it to one of his Sunday services when he resurrects Grace of God, which I have no doubt he will.

What the hell. It can't be worse than the sermons I suffered through as a kid. And at least, whether I agree with him or not, this guy walks the damn walk.

Peggy asks me if I want some lunch, which seems to be a couple of delivery pizzas. I kiss my old mom good-bye and tell her I'll have to take a rain check. I have one more interview on my dance card.

CHAPTER TWENTY

I've been in the lobby twenty minutes, chatting with the guard, when I see Big Boy Sunday's Explorer roll up outside. His driver parks in the handicapped space out front. The guard gets up to make him move. I tell him I'll take care of it.

I go outside and ask if they can park on the other side of the street, suggesting it might avoid some kind of incident, such as Big Boy's seventeen-year-old knucklehead chauffeur pulling heat on our superannuated protector.

"The excitement might kill the old man," I tell Big Boy, who grunts and tells the kid to move it.

"Be back in half an hour," he tells him. "Go on."

The kid gives me the stink-eye but does as he's told.

Instead of having a chat in our lobby, where Feldman is likely to appear at any minute and want to join the conversation, I guide the big man over to the elevators. The guard is looking very uneasy. If anybody ever looked out of place, it's Big Boy Sunday in the Prestwould. I give the guard the "OK" sign.

"Where we goin'?"

"Up to my place."

"You live here? Shit. What'd you do, win the fucking lottery?"

"It's a long story. I'm renting."

We get off at six. Our neighbors, the Garlands, are out of town, and Custalow is at work, somewhere down in the basement.

"Nice view," he says, looking out across Monroe Park at the cathedral. He asks me how much a place like mine costs. When I tell him, he says that doesn't sound like much. Then I tell him about the four-figure condo fee.

He whistles and allows that he'll stay where he is for the time being.

I ask him if he wants a beer. Maybe I should have made a little light lunch. My manners are showing.

He declines and looks at his watch.

"So," he says, "what'd you get me up here for? Better make it quick. My boy is going to expect me out there in, uh, twenty-five minutes."

Time to cut to the chase.

"I told you I found something when I was in Alderman's place."

I walk over to the mantel and pick it up. I hand it to him.

He looks at the gum wrapper.

"Teaberry," I say, stating the obvious. "Nobody I know chews that crap, except you."

"So what?"

"Nothing much, except there it was, lying on the floor there next to the trash basket, like somebody aimed and missed. I guess the cops didn't think it was important. And, to cap it off, there was a piece of gum inside. I saved that though. It's in safe hands."

Big Boy sits down. He's got the gum wrapper in one of his big paws.

"So, you shakin' me down, or what?"

I tell him I don't roll that way.

"I just want to know what the hell happened," I tell him. "From all the interest you've had in this mess, and from that gum wrapper, and from knowing your reputation, and from knowing Artesian's momma is your woman, I'm doing a little deducing."

I have considered my options. The one that would not have labeled me a potential suicide would have been to go to the police. That gum might be DNA-able, and Big Boy Sunday is more than capable of doing what was done to James Alderman.

But I'm not quite ready to turn this over to L.D. Jones, whose minions somehow missed it in the first place. This one is mine.

Of course, I also could have just pretended I never saw that Teaberry gum wrapper. As with going to the cops, it would have improved my chances of making it to retirement.

But, dammit, I want to know what happened. And I don't want to get it secondhand, from some police report or through the back door via Peachy Love. This is my story. I'm betting that the fact that I've sent those two letters will be enough insurance to get me through this in one piece.

Plus, as Big Boy and I both know, some people just naturally fall into the "Needed Killing" category.

"Just tell me what happened."

Big Boy looks at his watch again. He sighs. Then he calls his driver and tells him to go get something to eat, that he'll call him when he wants him.

"Go by KFC," he says. "Get a bucket. Extra crispy."

Always thinking about the food. I knew I should have done the light lunch.

I sit down next to Big Boy.

"If I was going to the police, I'd have done that already." He nods.

"But there ain't no way you're going to get something for your paper out of this, unless somebody hauls me off to jail."

It's hard to explain that I just want to know. This one's gotten under my skin, and I want answers. I want the final piece of the puzzle.

"They're goin' to pin it all on Alderman anyhow," Big Boy says. "They got the bodies. What do you care who put him down?"

"And can they tie Artesian Cole's murder to Alderman?"

He gives me a long, withering look.

"The people that need to know, they know."

I tell him I'm not wearing a tape recorder and I'm not toting a note pad. I tell him it's not for attribution.

What I'm betting is that Big Boy Sunday got a lot of information out of James Alderman before he put him out of his misery. That's what I'm after.

"Shit, you can't tell this story without somebody knowing who you talked to."

I assure him that I can. I also assure him that I have never revealed a source and never will, even if I have to go to jail.

He looks at me.

"Yeah, you'd last about ten minutes in jail," he says.

I tell him I've been there before. Sure, it was only for a couple of days, and the subject was a state official taking a bribe, not a spectacular murder. But I didn't blink, and the prosecutor knew I wasn't going to.

Finally he puts his big, pink palms up.

"You think you know shit," he says, "but you don't."

He gets up and wanders over by the gas-log fireplace, backing his oversized butt up to it.

"You know who else chews Teaberry gum?" he asks. "Shorty Cole, that's who.

"He started chewing it just because I did, I suppose. Your mouth's open, Willie. You ought to close it before you catch flies."

I do as he suggests. As is so often the case, I am not as smart as I think I am.

"So tell me."

And so he does.

Big Boy might have put more resources into finding out what happened to Artesian than the police did.

"I know people," he says. "Some of them are out there on the street, and they don't miss much. I had my boys snoop around, and they found a fella that the cops never found. One that doesn't like to talk to cops even when they do find him.

"This fella saw something. He said he saw a black boy get into a big-ass car, over there just off Broad, about the time the boy would have been leaving that place on Grace, headed home. Said the car was old as shit, like an antique. But this fella, he knows cars, used to work for a used-car dealer. He said it was a Ford Galaxie, burgundy and white. I thought it couldn't be. Hell, they quit making them in the 1970s. But the fella was sure."

I know, because I saw it, that there was a Ford Galaxie parked in James Alderman's garage. Burgundy and white. It was easy enough for Big Boy, with his official and unofficial connections, to trace an antique car to Seminary Avenue. It was easy enough to discover Alderman's connection to Children of God.

"I was going to bring the wrath of God down on his
sorry-ass head," Big Boy says, "but Shorty beat me to it."

He had made the mistake of telling the boy's uncle what
he found. That was on the Thursday after Artesian's body
surfaced.

"But I swear to you, I was going to do it by the book.
I don't need that kind of attention. I figured I had enough
information that I could pass it on to the police. I got a few
friends down there. And then I'd let them take care of James
Alderman. I figured he'd suffer more from being exposed for
what he was and having to spend the rest of his life in prison
than he would have suffered from somebody torturing him
to death."

Big Boy makes a noise that sounds like a chuckle.

"Although, I must admit, Shorty did a pretty good job."

I ask him if he or Shorty knew about the other boys.

"Hell, no, at least not right then. I knew about how the
kids would talk about Frosty this and Frosty that, but I didn't
know for sure if there was a real Frosty. Even when it popped
up again after Artesian was killed, I wasn't sure there was a
connection. Kids disappear sometimes, where I live. All Shorty
was there for was to get payback for Artesian."

So Shorty Cole found out who almost surely raped and
murdered his nephew the Thursday after it happened.

According to Big Boy, Shorty didn't go ballistic.

"If he'd of said he was goin' over there and carve him up,
I'd of stopped him. Like I said, don't need that kind of trouble, and the courts would have hurt him more than Shorty
did."

Shorty Cole told Big Boy all about it the same day they
found the body.

The day before, he had slipped into James Alderman's residence while the old man was at his gym.

"I didn't know Shorty had it in him," Big Boy says. "But if you get mad enough, I s'pose all bets are off. I wasn't happy he did it, but he was entitled."

He said Artesian's uncle still had blood on his clothes when he came by Big Boy's house to tell him what he'd done.

Considering that Shorty was upset enough about his nephew's disappearance to brandish a gun at our publisher, I guess I could have seen this coming.

Shorty told Big Boy it was pretty easy. Pretty easy, I'm thinking, if you don't mind butchering another human being.

He tied Alderman up and started working on him.

"He said he didn't cut anything off until he got the man to confess. Shorty has a strong sense of right and wrong. But he said it didn't take long. And then Shorty started whacking away."

Alderman told Shorty about picking up the boy, and about strangling him later and then putting him in a sack and driving that same Galaxie over to the park after dark and dumping him in the lake. He said it was pure luck that he happened to be driving along that street at the same time Artesian was walking toward the bus stop. Since the boy knew him, it was easy enough to get him into the car. And it was easy to convince him to take a short side trip to Alderman's house to help his soon-to-be murderer move a piece of furniture.

Admitting he'd sexually molested the boy took a little more persuasion, but Alderman finally owned up to that too.

Shorty asked him the sixty-four thousand dollar question: Why? Alderman apparently couldn't give him a satisfactory answer, even after Shorty had cut off the first of his thumbs.

"Shorty said he said it was just something he had to do. He said he never did it unless opportunity knocked. I guess he was talking about those other boys. "Shorty said he actually grinned at him and said the devil made him do it. Said it spooked him out."

I ask Big Boy if Laquinta knows what her brother did.

"I expect she does. But we'll all be better off if we never talk about it. It's not like she can take out no ad in the paper: 'Congratulations to my brother, Belman Cole, for avenging my son's death.'"

I'll have to pass this information on to McNish some day, when I'm confident I can trust him to keep it to himself.

"I asked him if he made sure he didn't leave any fingerprints or anything. He said he didn't, but if he was dumb enough to throw that gum wrapper at the trash can, and miss the son of a bitch at that, I guess anything's possible.

"But you know what he said? He said if he did life in prison, it'd still be worth it."

There are so many things I want to ask Shorty Cole and Alderman. Cole's the only one who got to interrogate the son of a bitch. For now, I'll have to get my information secondhand.

"Why did Alderman dump Artesian in the lake? Why didn't he just bury him like the others?"

"Well, you got to remember, Shorty didn't know about no 'others.' But you were down there. I read your story. Sounded like that little basement graveyard was pretty crowded.

"I think the son of a bitch just flat ran out of room."

Big Boy looks over at me.

"Well, Willie. Now you know what you know. The question is: What are you going to do with it?"

I tell him I don't know, but that whatever I do, it won't have his or Shorty Cole's name on it.

He seems to take me at my word.

"You got some trust points with me. The thing is, don't waste 'em. I like you, Willie. I'd hate for anything to happen to you.

"Plus," he says, "you're a brother, even if you are a tad on the pale side."

He makes a call and asks his driver if he's picked up that chicken like he was supposed to. He tells me he can let himself out.

It's the most frustrating thing in the world for a newspaper reporter to have information this good and not be able to put it in print. It's like winning the lottery, but you can't tell anybody about it or spend the money.

But there are some impediments to putting the truth in print.

First, I imagine that if anything police- or courts-wise happened to Big Boy or Shorty because of something I wrote, I or my near and dear would somehow pay the price. Big Boy Sunday has, according to reliable sources, filleted bigger fish than me when they crossed him. Plus, I've promised to keep Big Boy and Shorty Cole out of it.

The other thing is this: Murder is almost always a bad thing. Sitting on the kind of information I have now is almost always wrong.

But there are exceptions. I think about those kids' remains in James Alderman's basement, and I think about what Artesian Cole went through.

Maybe our feckless law enforcement personnel will finally figure it all out and arrest Shorty Cole for murder, just like maybe they eventually would have found that other basement room and all those graves.

They won't get any help from me on this one though.

I think about what Huckleberry Finn said when he finally decided that, no matter what, he couldn't turn Jim in.

All right, then, I'll go to hell.

CHAPTER TWENTY-ONE

Wednesday

I do have today off, which sort of makes up for yesterday.

When I finally got to the paper, my head was buzzing from the stories I was going to write and the one I felt that I couldn't. It was already three thirty. Sally Velez looked at the big clock on the wall, now draped in fake ivy. I told her I had a nice yuletide gift for our readers. I also told her that any dirt naps in our city might have to be covered by someone else.

The piece on Sam McNish was relatively easy. After all, I had an exclusive, with the interviewee's blessing. I touched on his background. I regurgitated what we knew already about the circumstances that led to his arrest. And I think, in all modesty, that I did a damn good job of portraying a man with a big brain and a bigger heart who was still reeling at the way he was betrayed but was determined to soldier on.

I wrote about his intention to keep Grace of God and Children of God going, at their present location or elsewhere.

"Sam McNish has Ivy League credentials," the story began. "He could have used them to become rich or famous or both. Instead, he chose to come back home and quietly make our little part of the world a better place. Now, he is coming to grips with the notion of pure evil. It is to his credit that encountering a devil has not made him think less of God."

I have McNish talking about how amazingly well he was treated by the other inmates during his time of unjust confinement. I shared snippets of the letters the kids and his flock sent him. I let him get on the soapbox a bit and rail about how many of his fellow prisoners were there for the kind of penny-ante drug crap that might get a white boy from the suburbs a few hours of community service and a stern talking-to.

Quite frankly, I thought I captured his essence. But I'm my biggest fan, so maybe I'm a tad biased.

I had to argue with McNish to get him to let me put a help box along with the story seeking donations to his ministry. I am hoping that the power of the press, which is now about equal to an aging hamster on a treadmill, can do some good.

When she finished reading it, Sally said it was pretty sappy, but she had to brush something that might have been a tear out of her bloodshot, battle-hardened eyes.

The second piece I banged out while Sally was tweaking the first one was a bit more personal, and a tad risky.

I recounted for our readers my short, successful career as a cat burglar. I summed up all the reasons I had come to suspect James Alderman of being less than saintly, especially the part where McNish remembered that long-ago dinner with the accused. I did not mention L.D. Jones's participation in the bought-and-paid-for whitewashing of Alderman's attempted abduction of Ray-Ray Soles all those years ago. After all, L.D.

didn't know Ray-Ray and his mother had been bought off. I didn't identify Ray-Ray either. I promised.

And I didn't mention the gum wrapper. At that point, I still wasn't sure what to do with the story that couldn't be told. The piece of gum, by the way, had been sitting on my mantel the whole time Big Boy Sunday was laying out his story. I couldn't resist.

There is a certain risk in announcing to your readers that you broke into a home, no doubt disturbing potential evidence. I am banking on the fact that L.D. notices the mercy I showed him and will return the favor. Hell, if he doesn't, I'll run another story, naming his ass.

My guess? The chief will issue a statement to the media, through Peachy. He'll decry journalists meddling in police matters. And then he'll let it drop.

First-person stories by reporters give me the heebie-jeebies. They smack too much of the kind of "look at me" journalism that some of my compatriots seem to prefer to actually digging and sticking to the facts.

But what do you do when you've put yourself ass deep into what you're supposed to be objectively covering? Well, sometimes you just have to say "fuck objectivity." I'm always troubled when I see some news snippet—the kind the local stations love to show even though it happened in Keokuk or Fresno—about some poor soul captured on some passerby's iPhone being swept away by floodwaters or screaming in pain after being shot. "Put the damn phone down and help him, you asshole," I have been known to rather loudly advise my TV. You have a choice between aiding a fellow human being and getting your anonymous bullshit "footage" on the evening news. How is that a hard decision?

But who am I to talk? It will be, after all, my byline on this "first-person exclusive."

And then there was the biggest dilemma. It was already six thirty when I filed the "I was a cat burglar" story and turned my attention to the story that seemed unwritable: How Shorty Cole came to cut the thumbs, balls, and dick off James Alderman in the process of killing him.

I knew what I came up with wouldn't totally please Big Boy Sunday, and it sure as hell wouldn't please my editors here, because there isn't much attribution. Irritating Sally further was the fact that I would not divulge a couple of names she felt any self-respecting story had to have before passing it along to our readers.

I told her if we had any self-respect, we'd all have walked off the day we got the twenty-five-dollar Food Lion Christmas bonuses. I also told her that everything there was true. Trust me, I said.

So the final story in our Christmas Eve trifecta told our readers how a reliable source had told "this reporter" about the way James Alderman died. It was mostly all there: the eyewitness who recognized the color, make, and model of Alderman's car, the unnamed individual who was able to trace it to the Seminary Avenue address, the grim scene inside the house as Alderman was tortured and screamed for mercy before finally admitting to being a monster.

The way I covered my ass? I lied. I wrote that this information came to me by way of an anonymous phone call on one of those cheap-ass cells that drug dealers use and then throw away. I said the caller didn't name names.

I don't see how the cops could trace any of this to Big Boy Sunday, even though they might suspect him, considering who his girlfriend is. And I sure as hell don't see them stumbling on the real killer.

But I started getting cold feet about eight fifteen, as I was finishing up my masterpiece.

So I took a chance. I called Big Boy.

"You need to meet me," I said, and I told him what I was about to do.

"I want you to read it," I told him, "and if you don't want me to, I won't run it."

He was in the middle of a Christmas party and sounded a little bit too jolly, but he agreed to come by the paper.

"Meet me outside in ten minutes," he said.

I did a printout and headed downstairs, walking right through the lobby where Shorty Cole had pulled a gun on our publisher nineteen days ago.

Getting into Big Boy Sunday's tinted-window gas hog wasn't the kind of thing your life insurance agent would recommend, but this seemed the only way to do it if I was to get the story out there without having to dodge Big Boy for the rest of my natural life.

He had apparently carried a plate of ribs from the party and was working his way through them. I handed him the printout and he told the driver to turn on the overhead light. To my relief, he didn't tell him to drive away, although he left the engine running.

He didn't say anything. He was getting barbecue sauce all over the copy, and I saw his lips moving.

"So this is your story, what you're going to stick to?" he asked.

I told him it was, come hell or indictment.

"Well," he said, drawing the word out into three syllables while I held my breath. "I don't see no reason why you can't run that."

He had the partition between the front and back seats up so the lad up front couldn't hear us. "It'd be good for folks to know that he killed Laquinta's boy, instead of having to wonder about it."

He offered me a rib. I accepted.

I started to get out, almost free. I had one foot on the pavement when he put one of his big paws on my bicep and squeezed while I froze in midbite.

"Just remember, though," he said, "I'm right here. I'm like old Santa Claus, makin' a list. You all better be good, for goodness sake. Know what I mean?"

I assured him that I did. He told his driver, who still looked like he'd love to shoot me, to drive on.

And then, along came Dominick.

She was in the newsroom when I got back upstairs with the good news that the story was, from my source's point of view, a go.

She looked like she had hitchhiked from Vermont. I found out later that she had had to spend the night in some cheap-ass motel near the airport in Burlington and then got stranded again at LaGuardia. Then she had to take a flight to the DC airport (I still call it National; kiss my ass, Ronald Reagan) and rent a car. And then the car broke down outside Fredericksburg.

She had come to the paper straight from the I-95, in the replacement rental car.

She did not seem imbued with the Christmas spirit.

"Why the hell didn't you answer my calls?" she greeted me. Other people in the newsroom had moved back into the shadows, away from me and Sally and out of the line of fire.

"And where the hell is Wheelie?"

I explained that my phone was on the fritz, just as the blues ringtone started playing in my pocket.

I turned off the phone and wished the publisher a Merry Christmas. Sally said Wheelie was taking his last two vacation days.

"Didn't I tell you you were fired?" she asked.

I reminded her that she was going to make it official when she got back.

"Well, I'm back. Now get the fuck out of here."

I told her, loud enough that the other, cowering staffers could hear, that I was sorry if I had screwed up the suits' plans to sell us down the river to a holding company, that if I had known that James Alderman's brother was one of the potential buyers, I might have backed off a little. (Bullshit, but I wanted the whole staff to know the score.)

I also told her that anyone defending James Alderman at this point might be tarred and feathered, and that, furthermore, if I came to grief over this, the whole English-speaking world soon would know that a publisher of a midsize daily newspaper in Virginia tried her level best to cover for a serial killer.

"We need to have this conversation upstairs," she said. She seemed to want me to lower my voice, which seemed unfair to me, since she'd F-worded me within earshot of a couple of dozen of my cohorts.

"No," I said, "we don't. And if you read tomorrow's paper, you might want to send me a goddamn thank-you note."

Rita Dominick, being the publisher, could have still sent me packing. She definitely could have told Sally Velez to kill whatever I was writing for today's rag. But she isn't stupid, or not always anyhow. She could see the handwriting on the newsroom wall, and she didn't want it to read, "Publisher quashes stories, fires reporter whose exposé killed takeover deal."

Lovely Rita is only our interim boss. She hopes to have a future elsewhere in MBA Land after she helps the money guys gut us and sell us. She probably can see that, if she's to have that future, I'd better have one too. At least for a little while.

"We'll settle this when Wheelie gets back," she said. Then she turned around and marched back out to her rental car and left us alone. I figured that she could read my story on her computer at home later.

Sarah Goodnight came out of the shadows. She walked up to me and planted a big one right on my kisser.

"When I grow up," she said, "I want to be like you."

I told her to be careful what she wished for.

And so here we are, all comfy-cozy on Christmas Eve.

Peggy, Awesome Dude, Andi, and young William are here, of course, as is Abe Custalow. And then we have Thomas Jefferson Blandford V, aka Quip, the man who would be my son-in-law if my daughter would allow it. Not sure how I want that one to turn out. And there's Sam McNish, who did a more-than-passable job of asking the blessing. Philomena and Richard Slade even drop by for a while, along with a host of neighbors.

And, to my great delight, we have the lovely Lucinda Peroni in our presence.

There are two tables with everything from chicken nuggets to a Smithfield ham that Cindy brought. There are ample half-gallons of bourbon and the makings for eggnog. Anyone walking by the window we've had to open to cool things off might catch a hint of cannabis in the air. I'm pretty sure McNish has been lured to partake. I even had a toke myself, a risky move since Rita Dominick is liable to start giving me daily drug tests in the hopes of getting lucky just once.

McNish is staying until tomorrow, when he's spending the day itself with some of his parishioners who want to welcome him back into their midst. He is going to give an off-the-cuff Christmas Day sermon at one of his flock's homes. He's already getting responses to the help box we ran this morning.

"One man," he says, and he names one of the city's most deep-pocketed benefactors, "said he wanted to give us twenty-five thousand dollars, no strings attached."

And they say nobody reads the newspaper. Maybe we should run a help box every day, on the masthead, in case anybody wants to give the newsroom a few bucks. It's bound to be better than depending on advertising or Christmas bonuses.

I thank Richard for putting in a good word with Big Boy Sunday and give Philomena a big kiss.

As for Cindy, well, she came with Custalow and me.

My Prestwould unit has, at least until I fuck things up, a third resident now. The master bedroom is plenty big for the two of us, and Custalow doesn't seem to mind. He and Cindy get along just fine, and the quality of food and general tidiness is sure to improve, although Cindy has made it clear that she didn't move in to be a maid. Since she's going to be chipping in on the rent, that seems fair.

I ran it past my landlady. Kate gave her blessing.

"Who knows?" she said. "Maybe the fourth time will be a charm."

Among the Christmas cards lying on the floor beneath my mail slot this morning was one without a return address or a stamp. Someone had somehow been able to get up to the sixth floor and drop it through the slot.

The card looked like one of the ones you buy thirty to a box at Rite Aid. Some would have called it politically incorrect, because it actually had a drawing of the nativity scene, and it said "Merry Christmas" instead of "Happy Holidays." Don't get me wrong. I'm all in favor of bringing in drones to take out those TV idiots who blather about the "war on Christmas." But, Jesus Christ, can't you call it what it is without employing some bland-ass euphemism?

It was signed "Shorty" and added "thanks for everything."
I imagine he's thanking me for helping him get a job. I
might never know.

Around eleven, I see that Cindy is fading fast. I gather
her and Custalow for the short drive home, promising Peggy,
Andi, and Awesome that I will be back tomorrow with a sleigh
full of goodies, especially for young William, who passed out
about three hours ago.

"He'd be just as happy playing with the boxes," Andi says.

I tell her I'm not doing it for him. I'm doing it for me.

Back at Chez Black, the three of us have a nightcap. Cindy
and I toast Custalow, unrivaled among friends and cotenants,
and then sack out.

"McNish asked me to come to that thing he's doing
tomorrow," I tell Cindy after we crawl beneath the covers.

"The sermon? Why don't we do that? Did you get the
address?"

I tell her I did, but that I don't want to do anything to
screw up my Sunday brunch tradition. She reminds me that
no place we ever go will be open for brunch tomorrow and
that, furthermore, it won't be Sunday.

I tell her we'll sleep on it.

She reaches beneath the covers and whispers to me that
she thinks "sleep" is probably just a euphemism.

CHAPTER TWENTY-TWO

Christmas Day

Christmas has seldom lived up to my expectations. As a kid, it seemed to fall into two categories. Either I didn't get what I wanted, which was the default mode, since the money Peggy made from a variety of low-paying jobs provided food, shelter, and little else. Or, if she would somehow manage to save enough to make my materialistic dreams come true, I'd be depressed at the end of the day when I realized that whatever followed Christmas was going to be a major letdown.

Damned if you do, damned if you don't.

As an adult, the coal in my stocking usually has been well earned. Too many Christmases have been spent in failing marriages or the aftermath of same. Too many times, I've preferred the company of fellow hell-raisers to that of those who are supposed to be near and dear. I have been drunk on the twenty-fifth more times than I've been sober over the last thirty years, and it usually is not a "Deck The Halls" kind of drunk—more like Scrooge if Bob Cratchit and his family had told him to take that Christmas turkey and shove it up his ass.

Regrets, I've had a few.

This one, though, has not disappointed.

Cindy and I were up at dawn.

She went out yesterday while I was shopping and managed to find a Christmas tree. I hadn't had one since the year before Kate and I broke up. Our last holidays together did not lend themselves to expressions of seasonal joy.

Granted, it isn't a great tree. Actually, truth be known, it's just about the ugliest damn Christmas tree I've ever seen. She got it at CVS. All the really good fake drugstore trees had already been taken. What we have is some kind of green not seen in nature. It has blue lights on it, like somebody in China thought blue was a good yuletide color. It's probably a blessing that half of them don't work. And it looks like somebody broke one of its scant branches. It's so small we put it on the coffee table.

I love it. I told Cindy we would keep it forever, as a symbol of our undying devotion.

She said she thought the tree's life expectancy was somewhat short of "forever."

We opened our gifts to each other, sitting on the couch. She got me two suits that are better than anything in my closet now. I bought her a coat and a couple of sweaters. The other gift she bought me was something of a shocker. It was a half-gallon of the kind of bourbon you should never mix with anything.

I must have looked surprised.

"I'm not your enabler, Willie," she said, "but I'm not going to be your disabler either. I'm not sure I'd be that crazy about Willie on the wagon anyhow."

"Just," she said, as she leaned over to kiss me, "try not to be an asshole."

I promised to try.

My other gift to her came in a fairly small box.

There was a reservation for two at one of those West Virginia ski resorts I've never been to but that Cindy claims she loves. I told her I'd go for the après-ski. And there was a small piece of paper inside.

"Just say the word," I had handwritten, "and I'll go to the jewelry store."

It seemed like a better way to proceed than doing the ring thing, considering my recent history. Offering a ring before you're sure it's going to be accepted could be painful. I was at a New Year's Eve party one time where a guy proposed to his date in front of about fifty people. He probably saw somebody do it in a movie. In real life, it didn't work so well. Talk about embarrassing.

She read the note, refolded it, and put it in her purse.

"When the time's right," she said, "I think we'll both know."

That seemed fair enough.

We packed the car and went over to Peggy's. It took the two of us three trips to bring everything inside, about two-thirds of it for young William. We spent a couple of hours opening presents and watching William grab at the wrapping paper and try to eat the bows.

Now, we say our temporary good-byes, promising to be back by early afternoon.

"You're going where?" my mother asks. I told her last night, but she's prone to dope-nesia these days.

"Church."

"Good God."

THE COUPLE who are hosting Sam McNish's return to the pulpit live out on the other side of Willow Lawn, on one of the many chopped-up pieces of Grace Street.

Their house doesn't seem that large, but it has a big-ass basement. The basement, when we get there, is full of folding chairs. They brought a lectern from somewhere. There are probably fifty people seated and a couple of dozen more standing where they can find a place. A few, including Cindy and me, are sitting on the stairs.

Sam doesn't talk long. He thanks everyone "for believing in me when it would have been easy to let so-called facts overrule faith." He reads a short passage from the Bible and talks about love and joy and other gifts he'd like to see everyone get. He says he believes the New Year will be the best one yet for Grace of God.

Looking around the room, I see believers. It has always scared me, how easy it is to get people to buy into a thing they can't see. I've seen so many people bilked by charlatans and turned into zombies in their desperate attempts to latch on to something that might last and make them whole. Like the bastards who scammed sinking homeowners out of their last few bucks with blue-sky schemes during the recent economic unpleasantness, they go around shooting the wounded.

Maybe, though, this time they have reason to believe. Maybe this time they won't get played for suckers. I want to believe that Sam McNish will treat them right.

The crowd is not all of one race, still something out of the ordinary in Richmond. And, to my amazement, there in the back of the room I see Laquinta Cole, sitting with her daughter and remaining son and dressed to the nines.

There's a piano down there, maybe borrowed just for this occasion. The congregation sings a couple of the hymns you only sing at Christmas, and then it's over. The whole service doesn't last fifty minutes.

But near the end, before the benediction, Sam says he has one more announcement to make.

He asks me to stand.

"This man," he says, "saved me. Without him, I would still be in the city jail. He believed in me. He had faith."

He leans forward a little so he can look me in the eye.

"Willie Black," he says, "I have faith in you too."

I mumble something and wonder what the hell he means, then sit down.

I manage to wade through the people who want to thank me for getting their pastor out of the slammer and wish me well. It's something journalists don't experience very often. Frankly, it makes me a little uneasy.

I manage to catch Laquinta and her kids as they're walking out the door.

She thanks me too.

"You've done a lot for us," she says, "for our whole family, in this terrible time."

There isn't much I can say. I talk to a lot of people who have just been robbed of loved ones. Telling them things will get better or you know how they feel is a bunch of bullshit.

Outside, as I'm opening the car door for Cindy, I look over and see, leaning against the Explorer, Big Boy Sunday. Then I realize the little man with him is Shorty Cole. Shorty's still got a court date in January over *l'affaire Dominick*, but things could be worse. I wave from a distance. Shorty waves back. Big Boy nods. They must have driven Laquinta's family over here and then waited outside for them.

"Who was that?" Cindy asks.

I tell her it's somebody I want to keep happy.

By the time we get back to Peggy's, it's after one, and everybody's waiting for us before digging in.

"You did a good thing, Willie Black," Cindy whispers to me as they're passing the turkey around.

Maybe I did, I think, as I lean down and kiss the top of her head. Maybe I did.